SEASON OF MIST

a novella

by **Paul Finch**

*Top 10 Sunday Times Bestselling Author
of the Detective Heckenburg and Lucy
Clayburn series*

Season of Mist
Paul Finch

It was amazing how quickly the autumn closed in that year.

It seemed that one moment we were all sitting at the top of the Valley, bemoaning the last day of our school summer holidays, our shoulders singing with sunburn as we looked back on a heady two months of bleached grass, midge bites and baking heat, and then the next (one week later, in truth) we'd returned to the regulated world of school and school hours, getting up grumpily to face mornings that were suddenly cool and dewy, and only seeing home again as evening descended in mist, murk and apple-scented freshness.

It was 1974, and such a startling transformation wasn't uncommon at that time. We had a succession of very hot summers and very harsh winters around then, with little in between, which is unusual in England. But that autumn seemed to fall particularly early to me, and as it blew its cold breath across the land, and wrapped the woods in crinkling red leaves, a darker darkness followed in its wake, and the shadow that soon lay across our innocent community had the shape and dimensions of a monster.

1

My name is Stephen Carter. I was thirteen at the time and attended St. Nathaniel's Roman Catholic High School, Ashburn, and I had more reason than most to regret the passing of that long, hot summer. Apart from those lazy days spent down in the Valley, a verdant cleft on the edge of our industrial northern town, I'd made a new friend.

Dominic Blyford had always lived in our district, but prior to 1974 he'd attended private school somewhere and had never moved in proletarian circles like mine. I'd known who he was vaguely – his house was only a few roads down from ours, but I'd regarded him as a 'posh git' simply because of the way he spoke. Mind you, the rest of us weren't exactly rough. As I mentioned, my pals and I lived on the *edge* of town – in a kind of middle-management suburbia. Our grandfathers might have worked in factories or down the pit, but our fathers didn't. That said, we weren't wealthy enough to affect airs and graces. We still thought that having gardens instead of yards and owning a car instead of having to go on the bus everywhere now meant that we were reaching for the stars. We'd also kept our Lancashire accents and attitudes, because Ashburn is not a big town and its middle class and working class mingled constantly and contentedly, their influences rubbing off on each other.

I first got to know Dominic properly, or 'Dom' as I came to call him, because I made it my business to.

I was at the age when girls were just starting to interest me, and when word got around early that summer that Dom's older sister had come to live with him, and that she was a stunner, I found myself paying more than passing attention to the quiet and in some ways curious family from the house a few roads down. Dom was one of three boys. His brother Gideon was fifteen, and his oldest brother Clark was seventeen. Their names alone seemed to set them apart from the rest of us – this was an era when the majority of school-age lads were either Pauls, Peters, Johns or Stephens. Another unusual thing was that the Blyfords were the only youngsters I knew who had lost a parent. Their mother had apparently died when Dom was very young, so they lived with their father, who looked older than my grandfather did. He was a consultant psychiatrist for the local health service and had supposedly earned stacks of money from a lucrative private practise, which you could tell from their house. It differed hugely from the rest of the houses in the neighbourhood mainly because it predated the neighbourhood, and even now wasn't really part of it. Whereas ours were all identical three-bedroom semis, each with a box-like garage, a strip of lawn out front and an only slightly wider strip at the back, the Blyford residence was a large, rambling structure with a mock-Tudor façade and extensive gardens, which circled it entirely and in summer almost hid it from view.

Doctor Blyford looked ancient to me; he was probably only about sixty, but short and slim, with waxen features and snow-white hair that was never less than immaculately combed. He was always a distant, rather remote figure – like someone from another century. Even when he wasn't working, he favoured black suits, black ties, black leather gloves and heavy Gabardine coats. By contrast, the younger Blyfords were a more with-it bunch, and, generally speaking, were handsome and robust. Gideon and Clark were tall and athletic for their age, with thick brown hair and cherubic faces, which looked vaguely Italian. But Beth, their nineteen-year-old sister, was the real work of art.

Both in shape and looks, she had what I'd call the faultless female form; she was five-eight in height and trim, but with curves that to my young and eager eyes were the closest thing to perfection. Her hair, which was so black it was almost blue, hung to her waist when unfurled. Facially, she was a pre-Raphaelite goddess, with dark, compelling eyes, a perfect nose, a perfect pink mouth, and skin as soft and pale as cream.

Me and my closest pals – Pete Tugton and Gary Gray – had heard about her well in advance of seeing her. The day we finally *did* see her, it was the very beginning of the summer holidays and we were down in the Valley. Beth just happened to come wandering in our direction while out walking Sheba, the Blyford family's Alsatian bitch.

The Valley ran along the back of our housing estate. The River Redwater, a tributary of the Ribble, cut through it, winding south into the town centre, where it promptly became the recipient of all kinds of vile effluent from such poorly regulated plants as the Dye-works, the Bleach-works, the Malt-works, and so on. The name 'Redwater' was a source of great amusement in Ashburn, as most of the time it flowed a ghastly grey. A railway line also ran through the Valley, on the other side of the river from the housing estates; but this was an old branch line, which was now derelict and nothing more than an overgrown track-bed. As kids, the Valley was our favourite place to play. Certain sections of it, mainly down the bottom along the river, were fenced off and used as paddocks for horses, but the rest of it was wild, steep grassland studded with clumps of trees. Towards the Valley's west end, there was a wood filled with ancient, fantastically twisted willows, which we called 'Scubby Hollow'. This encompassed the river and was the point where a quiet lane, which was actually a narrow extension of my own road, Hill Bank Close, became a footpath and crossed to the other side via a footbridge. Few folk went over there these days, though at one time they had done. On the far side of the Valley, this path crossed the railway, then rose steeply uphill through more alternating bands of trees and pasture, wove around the small farmstead to which the horses in the paddocks belonged, and at last adjoined the immense sweep of spoil-land that had once been Ettinshall Colliery. This was a barren waste, which rolled on and on northward until it reached the M6 motorway, from where it was visible only as a moonscape of unsightly slag heaps. From the back of our house you could still see clutches of gutted buildings up there. I'd visited Ettinshall a few times, but it was on the extreme edge of our territory, and I hadn't enjoyed it much. It had a brooding, melancholy atmosphere, and it still possessed that burnt coke odour of the pit, which seemed to get into your throat and nose and clog your sinuses.

Anyway, on the day in question, which was a vintage July scorcher of the sort we rarely seem to get in this era of global warming, we were mucking about at the west end of the Valley, scrambling our bikes along the twisting paths of Scubby Hollow, or carving our initials into the trunks of trees.

And suddenly this amazing girl appeared, her dog trotting along in front of her.

We were struck dumb as she smiled and breezed past us. She was clad in a sleeveless white t-shirt, faded jeans and white plimsoles; she strolled idly, but with a gentle sway to her hips that was almost hypnotic.

"That's got to be her," Pete whispered. "Beth Blyford."

"Blood-ee hell!" Gary added. We'd only been in middle school a year and were still trying out those swear words and obscene phrases that fear of God's wrath had meant were a no-go area while we were still in primary school. "Blood-ee, blood-ee hell! Everything they say about her's true."

I was even more smitten than the other two. As a middle-aged man now, I look back on it and realise that Beth's most attractive feature was her naturalness. She oozed sex appeal, but it was effortless; she didn't need makeup or glamorous clothes. She was one of those rare, Eve-like creatures that nature occasionally casts up to remind the rest of us how far from the path of perfection we've strayed since Adam's original sin. Of course, at thirteen, I was too young to be sexually aroused by her. For me it was a purely emotional impulse, in fact an emotional *high* – brief but so intense that it left me physically drained, that my stomach simply flopped. I gazed after her as she receded along the path on the other side of the river, subconsciously aware how delightfully round her bottom looked in tight denim and knowing that I would never feel such exhilaration again – until I saw her the next time, and the time after that, and the time after that.

We're very irrational at that age. Like our house on Hill Bank Close, the Blyford house adjoined the Valley because it sat at the end of a residential cul-de-sac: Jubilee Crescent, which was an offshoot of Ashburn Lane, our town's main artery. So, if I wanted to see her again, it was far more likely that I'd do it at the bus stop where the two roads met, or maybe in the park a little further down Ashburn Lane, which she'd have to walk past if she was headed to the town centre on foot. But because the first time I saw Beth was in the Valley, she and that location became interwoven in my overheated mind, inextricably linked in the fog of my desires.

As a result, though the Valley was already our regular hangout, I now made a point of going there every single day. Unfortunately, Beth didn't. In fact, she didn't come down to the Valley again for the remainder of that summer, though I always entertained enthusiastic hopes that she might. Quite often this hope alone was enough to send me giddy. Then, one day in August, someone else came along who was probably the next best thing. I was perched half way up a tree at the time, inexpertly wielding a hammer as I nailed some rotten planks we'd found between a pair of parallel branches. We were in the process of creating a flimsy platform that we would later call a 'treehouse' and be immensely proud of.

"You're Stephen Carter, aren't you?" a voice said from below.

Peering down, I saw Gideon and Dominic Blyford staring up at me.

You'll remember that when I first mentioned the Blyford family, I called them a handsome bunch *generally*. That's because Dom was the exception to the rule. Whereas his older brothers were tall, he was short and stumpy – he would probably grow in due course, but there was no sign of it yet. Whereas they possessed a regal poise and bearing, he was awkward – he shuffled when he walked, slouched when he sat, and gawped when he was lost in thought. Whereas they were almost always coolly dressed, even when clad for the outdoors, he even looked scruffy in his school uniform or his Sunday best. His hair was a mop, and he smelled of biscuits – or so I'd heard, because I'd never got close enough to check for myself.

"Steve," I told them. "Everyone calls me Steve."

"Well Steve," Gideon Blyford said. "Dominic here wants a word with you."

I glanced at Pete, who was sharing the construction duties with me. He looked equally nonplussed. Shrugging and remembering to scowl because I wanted to make it look like this was an annoying interruption to our very important work, I swung down, hung by my arms from a lower bough, and dropped.

Gideon folded his arms as he surveyed me, determinedly unimpressed. "You go to St. Nathaniel's High, don't you?"

I nodded, brushing the dirt from my hands.

"We hear you're the cock of your year?"

I wasn't so sure about that and said so.

Gideon seemed surprised, as if such an admission was the last thing he'd expected. I was very soon to learn that he put great emphasis on his perceived notions of manliness.

"That's what we hear," he said. "Whether it's true or not, Dominic here is going to teach you a lesson."

At a nod from his older brother, Dominic unzipped his cardigan, shrugged it off and advanced towards me with his fists clenched.

10

Call me dim, but I still didn't know what was going on.

"You want to fight?" I asked. "Why?"

Dominic, who didn't look hugely eager, opened his mouth to say something but Gideon cut him off mid-sentence.

"Don't talk to him, Dominic, just hit him."

Dom came on, wide-eyed like a scared rabbit.

I suppose I should describe myself at this point. I was just under six feet tall and reasonably solidly built. I wasn't destined to grow much taller, but despite not being particularly fierce, such height at that age gave me a huge advantage. I was fit too, being captain of the school Rugby League team. So, when he swung a slow, wide punch, which I should have realised straight away was a reluctant one, I was easily able to dodge it, and clock him on the side of the jaw with a crisp left hook. That brought tears to his eyes, but at Gideon's insistence he persevered, trying to wrestle with me rather than box. I grabbed him around the waist, lifted him up and threw him down like a rag doll.

Pete dropped from the tree, watching the encounter with fascination but also puzzlement. Dom got up, dusty and dishevelled, and now openly crying, though this probably owed as much to humiliation as pain.

"He's got his mate with him," he protested to his brother.

"His mate's just watching," Gideon snarled. "Do him. Do him now!"

Sniffling hard, Dom came at me determinedly, arms windmilling. But having a much longer

11

reach than he did, I'd punched him on the nose before he'd even got close. It was no more than a jab, but it hit the right spot. The next thing I knew, Dom's hand was clutched to his nostrils, and mucus-filled blood was bubbling between his fingers. More tears spilled down his cheeks as he sank to his haunches.

I lowered my guard. The fight was over.

"Dominic, I've said this before and I'll say it again," Gideon stated flatly. "You're a disgrace to the family name." And he marched stiffly away, as if he'd done his best but was now washing his hands of the whole affair.

The dust was still settling. I gazed down at Dom. "You all right?"

He nodded, sniffling again.

"So … what was that about?" I was still bemused by the incident.

"Your school."

"Our school?"

"I'm starting there in September."

"At St. Nathaniel's?"

He nodded glumly.

"I thought you went to a posh school?" I said.

"I did 'til the end of last term."

"What's up?" Pete asked. "Your dad run out of cash or something?"

Dom's cheeks reddened a little. "Not at all … Dad thinks I should meet other kids – you know, kids who live round here."

"Why? You've never bothered before." Pete could be disconcertingly frank in the way he asked and sometimes answered questions.

Dom shrugged, flustered. "I don't know, it's a just a decision he's made."

"So, let's try and understand this," I said, "you're going to a new school, and the best way you can think to make new friends is to pick fights?"

"It was Gideon's idea."

"Bit of a non-starter really, wasn't it?"

He tried to get up and I helped him.

He glanced at me with surprise and no little gratitude. "Gideon said that if I managed to batter the lad who was the cock of my year, I'd have no problems when I got there. Everyone would respect me."

Pete chuckled. "Did you stop to wonder what might happen if the cock of your year battered you instead?"

Dom shuffled his feet. "It's Gideon. He thinks you have to stand up to people."

"Well you stood up to me," I said. "But he didn't seem that impressed."

"He's always trying to make me something I'm not."

"He probably wants what's best for you."

"Yeah." Pete hooted with laughter and leaned forward to check Dom's bloodied nose. "That's plainly obvious."

Even Dom saw the funny side of that. "My name's Dominic Blyford."

"I know," I said.

"You do?"

Again, he seemed surprised and even grateful, so I didn't mention that I'd always known who he was mainly because he was a figure of fun, or because I now knew him for another reason, namely that he was brother to the gorgeous Beth. I must admit, the thought of Beth was at least partly the reason why I was being so friendly to him: I didn't want her hating me as the guy who beat up her sibling.

"What you fellas doing anyway?" Dom asked.

"Laughing in the face of danger," Pete replied, indicating the treehouse.

"You'll not be laughing when that thing collapses with you on top of it."

"You got a crystal ball or something?" I said.

"I don't need one." He pointed up. "It tilts, look."

"So?" Pete got defensive. "One of the branches is lower than the other, that's all."

"Yeah, but that means all the weight is concentrated at one end, the one fixed on the right."

"And?" I asked.

"Well, the nails pinning the planks are coming down into the branch from the left-hand side, and at a deep slant. Even from here, I can see there's probably only about a centimetre of each nail embedded."

"Felt solid enough to me," Pete said.

"It'll only last a couple of days. What you need to do is put nails in from either side of the branch. That should secure it properly."

"You know about this stuff?" I asked.

"A bit. I used to be in the stage-crew for our school theatre."

"School theatre?" I mouthed to Pete. We'd never had anything like that; it sounded different and exciting. I turned back to Dom. "Come up and give us a hand, if you want. We've got a spare hammer, loads of nails."

I glanced at Pete, who shrugged but didn't seem totally pleased. Dom followed us up the tree via treads that we'd created ourselves through hammering bunches of nails into the trunk. He scaled these more easily than we'd expected – he might have been a weed to look at, but he was lithe enough.

"You could also put two nails in each plank at the point where it lies across the top of the branch," he said when we'd all got up there. "Make sure each nail is facing the opposite direction from the other. There'll be no give in it at all then."

I nodded, impressed. Pete just shrugged again.

What can you say about how surprisingly quickly some friendships develop?

I think it helps when the two people involved are consciously working at it. In Dom's case, the days were ticking towards the start of the new term, and he anxiously wanted an ally at St. Nathaniel's, which, being an urban comp, would probably seem a little 'Wild West' after the sedate institute he'd attended previously, whereas I saw advantage in getting to know him because it might bring me that little bit closer to his sister.

As such, Dom was soon a regular part of our gang. It transpired that he'd only been in the stage-crew at his former school for about two weeks and didn't actually know much about woodwork or joinery; he didn't know much about anything – unlike his brothers, he was a poor student. But he wasn't dense, he shared our sense of humour and he was enthusiastic for the rough play demanded by the big outdoors. In those remaining weeks of our summer holiday, we didn't just construct treehouses with him, but also woodland hides, bows and arrows that worked, and proper scrambling tracks around Scubby Hollow, complete with chicanes and hairpin bends. Gideon, who we saw more and more frequently, accepted the situation grudgingly. He'd still wanted Dom to insinuate himself into our society as the alpha-male, but perhaps deep down he'd realised this could never be. Soon, he was on reasonably good terms with us. Gideon was apparently an accomplished rock-climber, who spent occasional weekends in Wales or his native Lake District with his wealthy school-friends. On one occasion, he gave us some blue nylon climbing-rope, which, when we hung it from a high branch over the Redwater and inserted a trapeze-like stick through its lower end, became the ultimate swing.

Inevitably there were casualties along the way. One such was Pete, who'd probably been my best friend during early childhood. In appearance terms, Pete was short and squat, with a freckled face and messy thatch of orange hair. He was something of a toughie, but given to possessiveness, and he found Dom's sudden arrival intrusive. He became surly, almost jealous.

And it wasn't as if I could whisper to him that I'd only befriended Dom to get close to his sister, because by then I genuinely liked Dom and enjoyed his company, and getting close to Beth – which hadn't happened yet – would only be a bonus. I was still an acquaintance of Pete's by the time we got back to school in early September, but our close friendship had cooled a lot. Gary, on the other hand, was more welcoming to the new guy. Gary had a long, ungainly body and even longer, even more ungainly limbs – when dancing at school discos he looked ridiculous, like a stick-insect on drugs. To complete the comical picture, in an age when most of us sported hair down to our collars, he wore a permanent short-back-and-sides that was a rather disgusting mouse-brown colour. Otherwise, he was totally nondescript, the archetypical average Joe (if a little taller and lankier than most), but an all-round good egg who quickly extended his obliging nature to Dom.

This was a positive, because over the next few months all the teenage boys of Ashburn were going to need to stick together very closely indeed.

2

"Heard about the murder?"

It was the Friday of our first week back at school. Dom who, rather fortuitously, had ended up in mine and Gary's form (Pete was one form down), still stuck to us like glue when out in the schoolyard, so we were all together.

"Heard about the murder?" we were asked again.

This was Colin Lapwing speaking; he was the school megaphone, the newswire, the gossip merchant. Many was the time he'd bellow across the yard as soon as he saw you and come racing over to feed you some completely uninteresting piece of tittle-tattle, though on this occasion there was more for us to get our teeth into.

"What murder?" I yawned, not at all convinced there'd actually be one.

Colin Lapwing was also given to embellishment. Once, he'd told me that a leopard had escaped from the town zoo, when in actual fact it was a muntjac. On another occasion, he'd informed an awe-stricken schoolyard crowd that the town's main supermarket had opened early that morning to be found so full of cockroaches that staff walking around in the dark thought they were stepping on spilled breakfast cereals; the truth was that his uncle, who was an exterminator, had been called to the cellar there, and had removed three.

It was one of those increasingly cold, dank mornings, and our breath steamed. I started that day's timetable with double-maths followed by double-French. I didn't think I could take much of Colin Lapwing's nonsense at this particular moment.

"A lad from St. Bart's," he said in a 'how cool is this' tone. "Found on a playground near his house late last night. He'd literally had the shit beaten out of him."

I eyed him curiously. Colin had a mop of white-blond hair, plump cheeks and bug eyes which seemed to entirely fill both lenses of his pebble-thick specs. For once, the startled look on his face appeared to be in earnest.

"A lad from St. Bart's?" I said. "What's his name?"

"Dunno. But he didn't come in last night, and the bobbies got called. They found him five minutes from his own house. Battered to death."

We pondered this in thoughtful silence. St. Bart's, or rather St. Bartholomew's, was the next high school along to ours – it was only about two miles away – and our main rival when it came to sport. While St. Nathaniel's teetered on the edge of the town's poorer district, St. Bart's catchment area delved deeply into it, so it had a reputation for being a tougher, more disorderly place than ours, though our school's Rugby League side would have challenged that assertion, having walloped them regularly on the field of honour.

Even so, despite the differences we had with St. Bart's, one of their pupils being murdered was a little too close for comfort.

Later on, the story was confirmed for us by one of our music teachers, Mr. Sankey. He was a squat, elderly man who seemed to live in a permanent state of angry frustration, mainly I suspect, because so few pupils were interested in the subject he taught. He was the only teacher we had who still wore one of those old-fashioned black capes over his leather-patched tweed jacket. He constantly puffed on a pipe as he walked quickly around the school, and rarely did more than grunt if you asked him anything outside his lessons, though on this occasion he had no choice. He'd half-stumbled while descending a flight of steps and had dropped a pile of sheet music all over the floor. Though we were on our way to class, a few of us stopped and gave him a hand, for which he was grouchily thankful.

"Is it true, sir, that a lad from St. Bart's has been murdered?" Colin asked.

Mr. Sankey glanced at us uncertainly. "Yes, I'm sorry to say, that is indeed true."

"Who is he?" Pete asked.

"I don't know the boy, myself. I believe his name is Dean Stanton."

None of us knew him either, though Donna Jarvis said she thought he might live near her grandma.

"I'm afraid I haven't got any further details," Mr. Sankey added, shuffling his papers.

"Who murdered him?" Dom asked.

"I suppose if I knew that I'd be onto the police right now, would I not, Mr … what's your name again?" He gazed at Dom, puzzled.

Dom explained who he was and that he was new, to which Mr. Sankey *harumphed* as if this was only a vaguely acceptable response.

"Don't they have a clue?" Colin asked, always keen to know more. "The bobbies, I mean."

"I'm afraid I'm not party to any information of that sort, Mr. Lapwing. Suffice to say it'll be some demented person, some monster who, because he spent his entire youth sitting at the back of the class sniggering and doodling in his exercise books, has now found that he can't get a job and as such his entire world has fallen in on him. Let it be a salutary lesson to you all."

And he perambulated away, puffing hard on his pipe.

A *monster*, he'd said. We knew what he meant – it had been a metaphor, not a description of reality. But it was disconcerting all the same to young and imaginative minds. When we got home that night, we found further details in the evening paper. A quote from our local police chief described the incident as: "Frenzied and barbaric. One of the most savage and wicked murders he'd ever come across. An act of utterly *inhuman* cruelty."

3

There had long been rumours of a monster living in our corner of town.

I know that for a fact, because I started them. I should qualify that statement – I didn't start them from scratch. It was actually my grandad who started them. A World War One veteran, former coal-face worker and infamous teller of tall tales, he was now dead but had been a permanent fixture throughout my early days and had liked nothing better than to fill my eager ears with his unique brand of homespun fairy tales, all flavoured with the smoke and soot of the industrial North.

'Red Clogs' was the one I remembered best.

According to my grandad, Red Clogs had been a collier who got buried alive during a cave-in. His mates dug frantically to get him out, but all the time rubble kept raining down, and soon it became apparent that the entire seam was in danger of collapsing. Some panicked and ran away, but his closest friends stayed. They worked tirelessly, and eventually thought they'd uncovered enough of him to pull him clear – but he was lodged fast. They kept digging, and finally found the problem: a heavy steel girder was lying across his feet, pinning him down. Meanwhile, a little further along the tunnel there was another roof-fall, and then another. The foreman decided that they had to take drastic action. The only way to get their pal out alive was to cut his feet off, which grisly act they performed with a saw. None of these men were surgeons of course, and they had no anaesthetic available. It must have been an unimaginably horrible scene, with the heat and sweat and blood, and the black dust and flickering candlelight, and the grinding of steel teeth through bone and cartilage, and screams that would have put the souls in Hell to shame.

But it worked – to an extent.

They got the poor man loose and carried him to the surface, and only seconds later the seam did indeed collapse right behind them. Unfortunately, by the time the cage rose to the winding-house, the dreadfully injured man was dead – he'd expired through blood-loss. Needless to say, it was seen as a great tragedy and no-one was held to blame. But over the next few nights the men involved were to receive alarming visitations. The foreman was the first. It was a Friday evening, and he was making his way to his favourite hostelry, taking a shortcut down a narrow backstreet, when he saw a figure standing beneath an arch that he had to pass through. Something about this figure stopped him. It wasn't just that it was shadowy and shapeless, but that it was sparking its clogs on the cobbles – and those sparks "burned with an evil red flame". Frightened, the foreman fled back the way he had come and spent the rest of the night with crucifix in hand. Another man was in bed the following night, when he was woken by what sounded like someone performing a complex clog dance down the alley behind his house. His hair prickled as he listened to a pair of steel-shod clogs come clattering into his rear yard and attack his back door, slamming repeatedly against the wood. Only in the morning did he find the courage to go down and look. What he saw gave him a seizure: extensive damage to the door, and bloody footprints all over it.

Similar things afflicted all the men involved. I forget the exact details, but my grandad swore that it was true, insisting it had happened back in the 1930s when he himself was working in the coalmines. Anyway, that was the full gist of the story. There was no resolution to it; it was more anecdotal than urban myths are today – which was where *I* came in. The only part of this demon that was actually corporeal, I decided, were the severed feet, which naturally were still encased in a pair of battered, blood-drenched clogs. The rest of it – its body, legs, arms, head – was basically a shadow form, a nightmarish outline, as black as coal itself and as cruel and wicked as the winding, airless tunnels from which it had been torn. Anyone was fair game for it. You didn't have to be one of its former colleagues, or even have a connection with the pit at all. This thing was now part of the ruined landscape, a predator of the spoil-land; it prowled during the darkest, coldest hours, brutalising with steel-shod soles any poor creature that stumbled across its path.

You may not be surprised to learn that I was regularly top of my class in English, and that at one time I had ambitions to earn my adult living as a writer of fantasy. But this creation had been

24

one of my better ones even by those standards. With the waning of each year, the Valley and its surrounding environs changed from a leafy, summery paradise to a place of mud, mist and naked, twisted trees; especially Scubby Hollow, which on occasions like that seemed the dreariest, loneliest place on Earth. Many was the autumn night we'd sat at the top of the slope in the safety of the street-lighting, and I'd held my young friends enthralled with my vision of a spectral shape creeping through the darkness below. "Though it isn't totally solid," I always reminded them, "it can still kick you to death."

It was ironic then, that a full two weeks had passed after Dean Stanton's murder before anyone put two and two together and came up with five.

It was during his funeral. All the pupils of both schools had been lined up for miles on either side of the main road leading to St. Bartholomew's Church, to pay their respects to the passing cortege. No doubt it was a sombre occasion, but to us youngsters it was a novel event and therefore interesting rather than sad. We, in our distinctive black blazers, were on the south side of the road, while St. Bart's, in their even more distinctive purple, were on the north. We were placed one pupil every five yards or so, each one of us facing an opposite number on the other side, which, as you can imagine, led to much mee-mawing and Mickey-taking. It seems a bit irreverent, but we hadn't known Dean Stanton personally, and the St. Bart's kids on our stretch of road presumably hadn't either because they gave as good as they got. Gary said he thought it was like a Mafia funeral, so we all started adjusting our ties and collars and frowning menacingly. Dom mentioned that if everyone in China lined up like this, it would go all the way around the world, which led to yowls of disbelieving laughter. He insisted it was true because he'd read it in *The Daily Mail*. The fact that he read *The Daily Mail* led to further scorn, which confused him a little, though he redeemed himself by quipping that *The Sun*, which we all pretended we read, was full of tits because it was for tits. Only when Mr. Lord, our moustached and frizzy-haired PE master, turned up and slapped a few heads, did we fall silent again.

After what seemed like an age, the hearse finally passed. It was packed to bursting with wreathes and floral tributes. The procession of funeral cars that followed was loaded with people in dark clothing, all holding handkerchiefs to their faces. That solemnised the mood a little. The kids on the opposite side of the road looked paler, quieter. Perhaps they hadn't all known the poor lad personally, but they'd certainly have seen him walking around and would have heard him speaking. The sight of his coffin must have brought this home to them much more than it did to us, for whom Dean Stanton was only a name.

While all this was going on, Mr. Lord was standing behind us, talking to one of our other teachers, Miss Manning, who we were certain he fancied.

"Have they released any details yet?" Miss Manning wondered quietly. "About the murder?"

Our ears pricked up. The gory details had been kept from us until this point.

"No yet," Mr. Lord replied. "But our Ben's just joined CID, and he reckons the lad was given a terrible beating, I mean like – all over his body. Some of the blows were so violent, they're thinking he might've been stamped on or kicked."

"Kicked to death?" she said, appalled.

"Or stamped to death."

"Good God."

Our hair stiffened. I caught Colin Lapwing's eye, and he mouthed something to me. I couldn't quite tell what he was saying, but he seemed to be pitching it more as a question than a statement. He mouthed it again and again, and finally I realised what it was: "Red Clogs?"

"Don't be daft," I whispered back. Only for Mr. Lord to slap the back of my head again and tell me that as I couldn't show the required respect there and then, I could show it on detention after school.

That evening, long after everyone else had gone, I walked home with Dom, who'd also picked up a detention thanks to his failure to deliver a homework project. He asked me who Red Clogs was; thanks to Colin Lapwing, everyone was now talking about it.

I found it a rather cool idea that my invented monster was creating such a stir, so I told him the full story without adding that most of it was fiction. When I'd finished, he pondered the tale

27

unhappily, and, oddly, I too began to feel discomforted. We'd been held back until nearly five o'clock, and it was a forty-minute walk home, which meant that it was now getting dark. Add to that the dank mist that had risen, and the quiet residential neighbourhoods we were cutting through, and suddenly we became aware how alone we were. At the time, we were strolling along a set of railings with some playing fields on the other side. The mist was particularly thick over there. In fact, beyond the railings we couldn't really see anything, and it was easy to imagine that someone – or something – was moving parallel to us, just outside the range of our vision.

And that was no fun. Whether I believed in Red Clogs or not, there was a still a murderer knocking around the district. But strangely, I was now wondering if maybe I *did* believe in Red Clogs. I hadn't made the story up entirely, and my mischievous grandad had always insisted that the bit he'd told me was definitely based on fact.

In the minds of children, fact and fancy can mingle quite easily, and back in 1974 we thirteen-year-olds were still children. We were physically tougher than thirteen-year-olds are today. We bore hardships without complaint and endured more severe punishment than could even be contemplated by youths of that age now, but we were less worldly, less adult in our outlook, far more naïve. All right, I'm not saying we completely believed in ghosts and goblins, but mysterious entities of that sort still lurked on the peripheries of our awareness, and it didn't take anything like as much as it would today to bring them out of the shadows.

And it wasn't as if our shock had been a mild one. Dean Stanton had been "stamped to death" in an act of "inhuman" cruelty, which only a "monster" would be capable of.

"I once heard a story like that," Dom said, subdued. "It was when we first moved here. I was too little to go out, but I remember Clark and Gideon being told to stay away from Ettinshall Colliery. It was still working then, but they were told not to go near the slag heaps because the spirit of a miner who'd been killed underground used to haunt them."

I was more than a little disconcerted to hear this. Ettinshall, which had still been in operation when I was very young, was the closest colliery to our house. Could it be that the Red Clogs legend had actually emanated from *there*?

"What was this spirit like?"

Dom shrugged. "I don't know. But they used to say that it wasn't some ordinary ghost that just went 'boo'. This was an angry ghost, and it'd come after you and try to kill you."

Not surprisingly, I was glad to get away from the railings and the fog-shrouded field beyond. By the time I reached home, darkness was falling properly and the part of the Valley that lay behind our house was a spooky abyss. It was therefore a great relief when, over tea, I heard my Dad talking to my Mum about the murder and saying the police had made an arrest. No-one was sure exactly who it was, but suspicions were rife that it was Dean Stanton's stepfather, a brutal drunk who'd given the boy and his mother a hard time for several years.

I was absurdly grateful for this. There was a mundane explanation after all, as of course I should have known there would be. We could relax, stop worrying and start enjoying life again. I went to school the next day in a lighter frame of mind – so much so that I never noticed the morning news bulletins, which reported that Dean Stanton's stepfather had been released without charge.

4

One of the things I particularly came to like about Dom was his singular uselessness.

I don't mean that in a scornful way, but he was wonderfully ill-equipped to survive in the rough and tumble world of 1970s youth. As I've already said, once you got past the general weirdness of his outward demeanour, he was funny and good company; but despite his undeniably adventurous spirit, he wasn't up to much physically. He would climb trees and build dens and swing out over the Redwater with the rest of us, but he often fell or got stuck. He wasn't up to much in a scrap either. As I'd seen on the first day I met him, he was usually prepared to have a go, because despite everything he still aspired to Gideon's ideals about courage and manliness (not that he had much choice, as Gideon constantly forced them on him), but it rarely had a happy outcome.

I'll give you an example. One day we were loafing about in the Valley, when a boy and a girl turned up in matching blue and white tracksuits. I highlight the tracksuit factor because it was unusual wear in those days. This was the period before designer labels and flash running gear. Most kids of our age were content to knock around in jeans, t-shirts and trainers. But these two, who were non-identical twins from a few streets away, were out-and-out sporty types, perhaps a year younger than us, but very confident and assertive. I didn't know them personally, but we'd seen them often: out jogging with Bertie, their pet Doberman, or cycling in perfect time with each other along the main road, which at that age seemed like a very daring and adult thing to me. I think their family name was Jacobson, though I never found out for sure. Colin Lapwing thought the girl's first name might have been Taluhla, which I didn't believe for one moment, especially as he also said the boy's name was Jacob – I mean come on, Jacob Jacobson?

Anyway, on the occasion in question they'd brought Bertie with them, as a result of which Dom felt he had to take Sheba indoors. Bertie would probably have been more interested in mounting Sheba than biting her, but, as youngsters, we didn't realise this. We got angry – at least, Dom did. Once we'd put Sheba in the house, we went straight back to the Valley, Dom insisting that we had to assert our ownership. The interlopers were still there, throwing sticks for Bertie. I must admit, even though Dom's immature outrage amused me, I partly understood it. Though the Jacobsons were just standing there, they were doing it with a proprietorial air. The Valley was *our* normal hanging-out spot, yet we'd had to go because they'd arrived. And now they were just standing there, unconcerned, bold as brass.

We descended the slope and Dom walked right up to them, laying the law down belligerently. There was much finger-pointing and wild-eyed gesticulating. He informed them that this was our patch, and that not only were they not supposed to come here without an invitation, but when they *were* here, they ought to treat us with the respect due to us, "not lord it just because they had a man-eater with them". He got so excited that the man-eater in question began to growl. Calmly, the girl instructed her brother to take Bertie away to a safe distance.

Then she turned … and took Dom out.

It was as simple as that.

The first blow was a punch, and it caught him clean in the midriff. He gasped. Then she slammed a knee into his groin, which doubled him over, before finishing him off with a karate chop to the back of the neck.

It was remarkable. She didn't waste any words on him; she didn't even waste any energy. Every shot was delivered with speed, precision and just the right amount of force. Dom didn't stand a chance. Afterwards, she blew a big bubble in the pink gum she was chewing, popped it, spat it out into her hand, and, bending down, plastered it in his hair as he lay grovelling.

"You'd better not say anything about this," he warned me, once the Jacobsons had sauntered off and he'd wiped away his tears.

"It'll be a bit difficult explaining to Gideon about the bubble gum," I replied.

We still couldn't get most of it out, even though we'd been trying for several minutes.

"I'll just say it was in a tree, and I walked past," he said.

"Yeah right, and he's going to believe that."

Of course, Gideon didn't. With that unerring ability he had to sense whenever Dom had lost a fight, he berated us for quarter of an hour, paying particular attention to me for not helping out. The story we'd finally admitted to was that Dom had been set upon by three lads. At Dom's desperate request, we never mentioned once that he'd actually been beaten up by a girl.

That was another thing so typical of Dom – others catching it on his behalf.

Not because he planned it that way, but because he was at times so inept that the results of his blunders tended to engulf everyone in close proximity. At school, Mr. Lord, whose genial 'Billy Connolly' looks belied the monstrous rage lurking inside him, used to reserve an especially severe chastisement for those fouling up in the gym. It was a kind of 'company punishment', like those practised in the British Army during Victorian times; the miscreant wasn't the only one who'd pay the penalty – his mates would too. In fact, when Mr. Lord was involved, the entire class would cop it. Very appropriately it was called 'Spartacus', and it involved everyone having to hang by their arms from the top of the wall-bars surrounding the gym. I hadn't actually seen the movie *Spartacus* at the time, but when I saw it in later years, I chuckled grimly at the memory of how other kids would come innocently into the gym to give Mr. Lord a message, and balk at the sight of groaning, sweat-soaked bodies crucified on all sides.

Even though it was only supposed to last for five minutes, it was an agonising experience. If anyone was caught trying to rest his feet on one of the lower bars, Mr. Lord would re-start his stopwatch and the ordeal would begin all over again; sometimes it could last up to twenty minutes. Dom earned us this draconian punishment three times in his first month at St. Nathaniel's; once for not having his kit, once for failing to complete twenty press-ups in thirty seconds, and once for swinging on one of the ropes and doing a Tarzan call.

But I liked him. Not necessarily in spite of all this – maybe because of it.

As I've said, he was basically one of the good guys, and endearingly daft. And who among us, if we're honest, wasn't daft? What about me? My interest in Beth, who was already a young woman of the world, was surely as absurd as any thirteen-year-old's interest in anything had ever been. Yet whenever I saw her, my stomach roiled. I went around to Dom's house at every opportunity in the vague hope she would be there.

It all seems very muddled to me now, these feelings of fun, friendship and infatuation, which so contrasted with the horror, revulsion and fear caused by that first gruesome murder. What was I thinking from one moment to the next? It's hard to tell. They say that after time you only really remember those moments of *extremis* – both the pleasurable ones and the painful ones. But there would be so many of both during that autumn of 1974 that I can't separate them in my mind.

I'm confident of one thing. As we forged ever deeper into that darkening tail-end of the year, and the nights got longer, and the rain got colder, and the mist was ever more thickly matted between the withering husks of bushes and trees, one sense should have started to supersede all others, even if it actually didn't – dread.

5

Our particular crowd loved the waning of the year. With the long summer days behind us, it would have been easy to sit indoors all evening, listening morosely to the rain patter in the darkness outside. But in our case, as October progressed, a totally different kind of fun invaded our world. To start with, there were three big adventures congregated in these final months, and the mere anticipation of each one was sufficient to leave us breathless with excitement. The first was Halloween, the second was November 5th, or Bonfire Night, and the third was the big one, the granddaddy of all seasonal feasts – Christmas. But these special occasions aside, that whole time of year was wreathed with an atmosphere like no other. You didn't notice it much when you first went back to school in September – the vegetation was still green then, if a little limper and wetter. But as night fell earlier and earlier, and the leaves turned crisp, and suddenly the mornings were misty and there were toadstools sprouting on every patch of soil, new opportunities arose that simply had to be exploited.

We'd always spend the first few weeks of the autumn prowling our darkened neighbourhood, scaling its fences and joyously pillaging its apple trees. There were also conkers to be collected. In those days, conker fights still hadn't been outlawed in the schoolyard, so we were able to set up our own leagues and knockout competitions. Performing well in these depended on having a large supply of ammo, and the Valley, which must have boasted more horse-chestnut trees than anywhere else in the borough, became a prime hunting ground. All through early October, it would be alive in the evenings with gangs of skirmishers scouring its leaf-strewn floors or battering its high branches with sticks and stones.

By mid-October, the atmosphere would have changed again. Dusk was falling before we'd even got home from school and Halloween was close, so we'd start to prepare ourselves for *ghostly* fun. Dare games were an ideal way to do this. Who would dare hide behind a wall and scare passers-bye by screaming as if he was being murdered? Who would dare walk down Hill Bank Close to the bottom of Scubby Hollow on his own? On one occasion Pete volunteered to do this – he was the only person I remember accepting this particular dare – and he agreed to take a tape recorder with him and tape his progress, thereby proving that he'd completed the task. Unfortunately, the tape was inconclusive. All you could hear on it afterwards was his nervous, rambling monologue, which, though it rose shrilly in tone the further down the Valley he got, and returned to normal on his way back, was no proof. The main reason to listen to this tape was for its finale, which, when he got back to the top of Hill Bank Close, consisted of a furious argument with the rest of us as we all cast doubt on whether he'd done it or not.

Routine games that could be played at any time of year would get a special autumn makeover. Hide and Seek became 'Werewolf by Night', courtesy of a Marvel comic strip we pinched the name from. In our version, the seekers were ravening werewolves who would snarl and growl as they hunted the others. It was scary as Hell but at the same time massively enjoyable. Another was Murder in the Dark re-titled 'Slaughter in the Dark', the person who was *it* claiming multiple victims instead of one.

Of course, all of this was only a prelude to the main October event, Halloween itself.

It's important to remember that in those long-ago days before its commercial aspects were exploited, Halloween wasn't such a big deal in the UK. There was very little on television about it, there were few organised events, the average person in the street might not even have heard of it. But our particular crowd was fortunate, because one of our teachers at junior school had been to college in America and had taught us all about the customs and traditions of that eerie feast.

This meant that when we had our annual Halloween party, we kids had to organise it ourselves, without the assistance of adults. It also meant that it wouldn't be indoors, but in a shed at the end of someone's garden. But the unofficial nature of these events, and the sheer crudeness of the preparation that went into them was part of their appeal. The fact that everything was rough and ready, that we'd all be in makeshift costumes, that whatever venue we'd chosen would be dark and dripping, stinking of mildew and lit only by the flickering glow of our jack-o-lanterns, and that we'd be far from the care and control of our elders should something go wrong, only served to fuel the spookiness.

In 1974, it was Dom's suggestion that we hold the party in the garage at his house. That seemed like a good idea to me. It was separate from the main house, at the end of a secondary drive, and surrounded by thick evergreen shrubbery. It didn't have any power connected to it, and even its wooden door, which was covered in flaking blue paint, had to be lifted manually to enable you to get inside. It also meant that we'd have to spend at least a few days around Dom's house, sorting things out, and that might bring me back into the orbit of his sister, who I hadn't seen for the best part of a month.

I know it sounds ridiculous: on one hand excitedly planning a childish party, and on the other lusting for the attention of a shapely, dark-haired nineteen-year-old. But these juxtaposed emotions were real. I was on the cusp of manhood and didn't realise it. We'd no idea that within a year we'd no longer be having Halloween parties in darkened garages, would have minimal interest in fireworks, and would view Christmas mainly as an opportunity to steal kisses from girls in class and sneak bottles of cider from our parents' festive stock. Perhaps that's one of the reasons why 1974 was one of the greatest and yet at the same time most terrible years of my life. I lived every moment of it with huge intensity, as though unconsciously aware that it was my childhood's last fling. Even now, so many years later, I remember every sight and sound of that last autumn of innocence, every star-spangled night, every mist-wreathed woodland, every twisted shape watching coldly from the shadows.

6

When we looked at it closely, Dom's house really was a spectacular location for Halloween night. The gardens, which were untended and deeply overgrown, though now desiccated by the season, were tangled, brown, and deep with mulch and fungus. The house itself, which was a tad dilapidated, was covered in moss and ivy, and, when all its thick drapes were drawn, no light penetrated out from it – it was your generic haunted mansion.

So, that was the spot chosen. Now on with everything else.

We clubbed our pocket money together to buy some black and orange silk, which we tore into strips to dangle from the garage ceiling, and kept all the best apples from our 'scrumping' trips so that we could put them in a barrel of water and bob for them. With our spare change, we also bought chocolate, which we cut to pieces and hung from elastic bands. The problem, as always, was where to get our jack-o-lanterns. Pumpkins weren't widely for sale in Britain in those days, and those few that were would have been prohibitively expensive. We normally used turnips, but these weren't cheap either, and melted candle-wax mixed with turnip flesh created a truly foul odour (besides, one undisciplined Saturday afternoon, we got carried away with our homemade bows and arrows and used the two turnips we had for target practise, shooting them both to pieces). So, this year we opted for tin cans. You may laugh but stripped of their paper jackets and washed out thoroughly, these made an excellent and much cheaper alternative. All you needed was a can-opener or a hammer and nail, and you could make all kinds of bizarre faces on them. We reckoned we needed at least twenty, but having left it late to reach this decision, we had trouble finding so many. Dom was able to produce a few, but as he was providing the venue, I volunteered to find the rest, something I only managed to achieve by rooting around in our dustbins.

It wasn't half-term yet, so we were still having to do all these jobs in the evening, and fit them in around homework, which, now that we were second years, was suddenly taking on a more serious aspect. It was thus around seven-thirty on a weeknight when I arrived at Dom's house with my sack of tins. The entire place stood in darkness, though this didn't necessarily mean there was nobody in. It was such a large house, with so many rooms both downstairs and upstairs, that light in one part of the building didn't always leak to the other parts; Doctor Blyford spent most evenings in the family lounge (which up to this point I had never been inside), with the curtains drawn on the window and a draft-excluder across the bottom of the door; if it hadn't been for the muffled sound of the television, you'd never have known he was there. But on this occasion, his big maroon Bentley was missing from the main drive.

I rang the doorbell anyway, just to see, and to my surprise it was answered.

Beth stood there. She'd only recently come home from work because she was still dressed in the smart skirt-uniform she wore on the cosmetics counter at Debenham's.

"Hello," she said.

"Oh … I, erm, hello."

She smiled. "You're Stephen, aren't you?"

"Erm, yeah. Hi."

"Are you here for Dominic?"

"If he's in."

"I'm afraid he's not. He's gone with his brothers and his dad to put some flowers on his mother's grave. It's ten years today since she died."

This possibly explained why Dom had been off school that day. Officially it was because he had a cold, but apparently his mum had been laid to rest in her home soil up in Cumbria, and it would take several hours getting there and back.

"It's okay." I offered her the plastic sack. "Can I leave these here?"

"Certainly." She took the sack, its contents rattling and giving off an aroma of spoiled food. She wrinkled her nose. "What are they?"

"Tins for jack-o-lanterns. For our Halloween party."

"Ahhh …"

"I haven't had a chance to wash them out yet," I said awkwardly. "I was going to do that tonight with Dom."

"Oh, I can wash them for you. Do you want to come in and wait? They should be back soon."

"Sure. That'd be great."

The interior of the Blyford house was a time capsule. All its furnishings were dark and heavy, and there was an air of faded grandeur. It smelled of dust, though it wasn't actually dirty. I think it's just that everything in there was old and used; a more discerning person than me might have spotted the odd strip of peeling wallpaper, the occasional patch of threadbare carpet. It also felt cold, especially at this time of year. I would later discover that the house didn't have central heating; the lounge benefited from a coal fire and could be warm as toast, but conversely, this seemed to intensify the chill in the rest of the building. A similar economy drive extended to the lighting. Lights were only ever switched on in rooms where family members were present. This was the case now. Beth had switched the porch light on to answer the door, but switched it off once she'd admitted me, and led me down a hall that was almost pitch-black. Not as familiar with the layout as she was, I had to grope my way along, and only saw her again when she opened a door at the far end, which connected with the kitchen.

I went in there with her, to be greeted enthusiastically by Sheba, who, from the outset of my acquaintanceship with the Blyfords had proved to be my friend. Beth bade me sit down while she pulled on a pair of rubber gloves. She was already half-way through washing the dishes, so she soon moved on to my stash of tins, wrinkling her nose again as she began to rinse them out.

"So, you guys are having a Halloween party?" she said.

"Yeah. In your garage."

"Oh, that's right. Gideon mentioned it. He's doing something for you, isn't he?"

"Yeah, he's got some sort of game lined up. Don't know anything about it, but he says we'll enjoy it."

"I'm sure you will. Gideon always gets stuck in with stuff like that."

I watched her as she did the washing. Her work uniform suited her admirably. It consisted of a white blouse, blue silk scarf and blue skirt, which, this being the early 1970s, was very short and very tight. She was wearing blue, high-heeled shoes; her legs, which were sheathed in flesh-toned nylon that *crackled* whenever she moved, were breathtaking.

"So, you and Dominic have become friends now?" she said.

"Yeah. It's funny. We only really got talking this year."

"I'm glad. He didn't think he was going to enjoy it at St. Nathaniel's, but he says that you in particular have made him very welcome."

"He's a great lad."

She glanced around from the sink, possibly unused to hearing such an opinion voiced about her youngest brother. "You're generous with your praise too. Well, we're all very grateful for what you've done."

If I'd been older and bolder, I might have said something like: "How grateful? Come over here and show me." But I was becoming tongue-tied. She was so gorgeous and so sexy – and yes, I *do* mean 'sexy'. Immature as I was, it was impossible not to be affected by her perfect shape and even more perfect poise.

What possessed me to say the thing I said next, I'll never know. I blurted it out without thinking, without even realising: "Do you have a boyfriend?"

She glanced around again, surprised. "Why Stephen … what a question!"

"What I mean is …" Suddenly I was frantic. I'd messed up in a big way, and desperately sought to cover it. "What I mean is … you can come to the party too, if you want. And bring him with you."

"Oh." She gave this some thought. "Well the answer to the question is yes, I do have a boyfriend. And though it's very kind of you to invite us, we have something else planned for Halloween Night."

I wasn't sure how to reply. Inexperienced as I was, I'd of course known that a nineteen-year-old would not want to attend a thirteen-year-old's party. I'd probably made myself look even more childish by asking her, but that was better than being thought nosy.

"You're not offended by that, are you?" she said.

"What? … oh no, no, no, no. Honestly, no, no."

She giggled. "Stephen … one 'no' would be sufficient. I speak English you know."

"Oh, right, yeah, course."

She smiled and got on with the washing-up.

I felt like the biggest fool in the world, but I also felt elated because I'd finally connected with her and found her as sweet a person as I'd imagined. I wasn't even disappointed by the boyfriend thing. I suppose I'd already known she'd have a bloke – how could she not, a catch like her? – but in my adolescent mind he wouldn't be much of an obstacle because when the inevitable moment arrived for me to prove my heroism, she'd be so bowled over that no-one would stand between us.

As it turned out, Dom and his brothers didn't return for ages, so I finally said goodbye to Beth and set off home in a dreamy state.

A thick fog had now come down, an autumn pea-soup typical of that era of coal-burning neighbourhoods, and you literally couldn't see more than four or five yards in any direction. I opted to head back via the network of residential streets between Jubilee Crescent and Hill Bank Close, rather than walk along Ashburn Lane. I'm not sure why – it wasn't much quicker. Perhaps I wasn't thinking properly owing to the luxurious half-hour I'd just spent. Anyway, it was extremely quiet. There was nobody else out, so at first, I thought the footsteps I could soon hear were echoes of my own – thanks to the fog there was an 'indoor' atmosphere. But when I stopped to listen, they continued. What was more, they *clinked*, as though whatever shoes were making them were shod with metal.

It was difficult to not suddenly wonder if they might be clogs.

I turned around, unsure which direction they were coming from. These were small suburban avenues; there was nothing sinister about them, yet the fog had rendered almost everything invisible. The houses and the cars on their drives were vague outlines. The lamplight filtering through curtained front windows was a spectral glow.

I walked on quickly. It might have been my imagination, but the *clinking* footfalls also seemed to speed up. Was someone abreast of me on the other side of the road? The fog was so dense that I couldn't see over there to check. I thought about doubling back to Jubilee Crescent and heading home via Ashburn Lane, which would be busier than this route. But suppose this person was behind me? It would take me right into their clutches.

I hastened along, my ardour for Beth diminishing as an instinct for self-preservation kicked in. Hill Bank Close was only a couple of streets away, but that suddenly seemed a considerable distance. In reality, all I needed to do was walk up a drive, ring a doorbell and tell whoever answered that I was being followed. But as a youngster you don't think logically like that, especially when you're scared. You just want to get home.

The footfalls were louder now, closer. And yes, those feet were definitely shod with metal.

Thanks to the acoustics of the fog, I still couldn't tell which direction they were coming from. Suppose it was from in front? I stopped short at that thought, but now blind panic was taking over. The inevitable soon happened – I ran, rounding the next corner onto Mulberry Road at reckless speed, and sprinting the remaining fifty yards to Hill Bank Close.

Whoever it was, they kept pace with me all the way. I risked one backward glance before I reached our house. Nothing was visible in the gloom, but as I shut the front door behind me, I had the sense that someone (or something) had been extremely close.

7

Halloween night started so well.

The laughs and scares were balanced perfectly – at first.

It was cold but clear. For once the vapours of the season had vanished courtesy of a strong wind, which had leaves skittering down every street and naked twigs clattering like bone fingers. Those attending were a select crowd. Aside from Dom and I, who were the organisers, there was Pete, Gary, and some other kids from school: Kevin Crumper, a burly rugby pal of mine, Colin Lapwing – who'd invited himself once he'd heard what we were planning, and two girls, Gaynor Jones and Sally Parker, who we all sort of half fancied. We also had to tolerate my kid sister, Sarah, who I'd been ordered by my Mum to take along, even though she was only nine.

Gideon had his 'special game' lined up for us, though he didn't show up straight away, and when he did, he hadn't bothered with a costume. In contrast, the rest of us had really gone to town. As the Hunchback of Notre Dame, I wore a rubber gargoyle mask and a ragged old coat, which I'd tied at the waist with a rope and shoved a pillow underneath. Dom was in vampire guise: he'd greased his hair, donned a black cape and wore white face-paint with fake fangs and red streaks at either side of his mouth. Gary was a straightforward ghost, wearing a white sheet with eye holes cut in it, though rather cleverly his mother had stitched the hood so that it stuck up in a klansman pinnacle. Kevin Crumper was the Frankenstein monster – all he needed for that was a mask, because, with his immense frame, massive squarish head and deep monotonous delivery, he was already three-quarters there; but he'd also put on old clothes that were two sizes too small and a pair of his brother's size twelve work-boots, to enhance the illusion. Gaynor was the White Lady, complete with a rotted old wedding dress, a rotted veil and white gloves blotched with green paint, while Sally wore a blood red cloak and a papier mâché pumpkin head. My sister Sarah was in black tights, a black leotard, whiskers and pointed ears, which made her into a rather effective black cat – this was largely thanks to my Mum, who'd also used coat-hanger wire and black cloth to construct her a tail. Even Colin had done the occasion proud, turning up as the Grim Reaper, dressed in a black cloak and armed with a plastic scythe. The only disappointment was Pete, who, by his own choice, had been less involved in this year's preparations and even now seemed indifferent. His simple clown mask suggested minimal effort.

We crowded into the garage, which, as well as the orange and black streamers, we'd furnished with deckchairs and lit with our tin jack-o-lanterns, which worked superbly; in that chilly half-darkness, their tiny, fiery faces grinned or scowled at us from every angle. To really get us in the mood, the night would start with scary stories. Everyone had to tell one. A few we'd heard before – apocryphal anecdotes like the couple who break down on a deserted stretch of road and the escaped lunatic who approaches their car after the boy sets off to get help, or the old lady on the moor, who is picked up by a kind motorist but then abandoned when the motorist gets spooked, and leaves behind a handbag containing a meat cleaver. From the classics, Gary recited *The House of the Nightmare*, while I chipped in with *The Monkey's Paw*. Gaynor regaled us with the lurid details of *The Exorcist*, which had caused a sensation that summer, and which her older sister had told her all about. Colin related a story which he insisted was absolutely true, and though I suspected he'd made it up on the spot, it creeped me out no end. It concerned a couple who were renovating a pub they'd bought, only to get disturbed by paranormal activity there; no-one would listen to them, but one night they disappeared, and all the police found in the morning were two voodoo dolls with pins in them – the couple were never seen again. The last story was due from Pete, who shrugged and said he hadn't really thought of one. Before anyone could criticise him for this, Gideon barged into the garage, telling us that it was nearly seven-thirty, and that he wanted to get on with the games as he was due to go out.

A dispute then followed about the bobbing apples. Dom said he didn't want to bob yet because it would wash his makeup off before we went trick-or-treating. The others argued that the trick-or-treating was best left 'til the end of the night because everyone could set off home once they'd pocketed enough money and not need to bother coming back here. Gideon stepped in and resolved the issue – everyone could bob for apples except Dom, and could we please get on with it!

The game went ahead with Dom watching glumly from the sidelines. He *was* allowed to participate in jumping for the chocolates on strings, only for his elastic band to snap loose at the top and whack him hard in the eye.

"Don't even think about crying," Gideon warned him from across the jack-o-lanterns.

We sniggered, until the same thing happened to most of the rest of us. On reflection, it wasn't a very good idea for a game, in the light of which I decided it was time we got out into the night before such semi-comical incidents changed the mood – we were all a little twitchy after the ghost stories, and I didn't want to lose that. Gideon rubbed his hands, pleased that at long last we were going to fall victim to whatever it was he'd been planning. In honour of a strip cartoon in *Shiver and Shake*, he'd named it 'Scream Inn'.

To appreciate Scream Inn, you need to understand the sort of gardens the Blyford house boasted. I've already mentioned that they circled the entire building. But have I described how deep and untended they were, how effectively their overgrowth concealed the nearby streetlights?

The front and side gardens were a profuse mass of foliage, separated from the house only by a narrow, paved path. But the rear garden, especially at night, was abyssal in its depth. It comprised three large lawns, which rolled away from the main house in a straight line, one following the other. They were divided from each other by thick holly hedges, each of which had only a narrow tunnel cut through it for access. All these lawns were overrun with ivy and briars, while the trees and bushes that fringed them were wild, unkempt and went back several dozen yards before reaching the perimeter fence. At the farthest end of the third lawn was something the Blyford family called the 'Spinney'. This was actually a small wood. It contained thickets and brambles rather than fully mature trees, but again it was dense and tangled. In summer it was matted with greenery, but in winter black and twisted like a chaos of gangrenous limbs. In the very heart of it, accessible by a winding path, was what they referred to as the 'Wendy House', but to call it the 'Eyesore' would have been more accurate. It was a small, timber structure, all elaborate cornicing and carved woodwork. It looked Germanic, like something out of Hansel and Gretel, and at one time had been painted jolly colours: pink, yellow, sky-blue. Now it was a sombre shell, drab and grey, every part of it riddled with decay. In recent times, the Blyfords had used it to store garden furniture, but with a leaking roof, no glass in its windows and mould running rampant throughout, it had become unfit even for this purpose. Viewed at night, it was an almost impossibly sinister sight, an impression reinforced by its remoteness from the Blyford house, or in fact from any other house.

There was another ten yards of thickets behind it, but on the other side of those was the rearmost fence, and beyond that the top of the Valley, a part given over to sheds and allotments belonging to the occupants of Grantham Terrace, which was the next road along from Jubilee Crescent, but still a good hundred yards distant. As Gideon led us from one lawn to the next, I had a growing sense of trepidation, which was not really helped by the claw-like grip my sister was keeping on my hand.

"This is not going to involve the Wendy House, is it?" Dom asked querulously.

"The rules are simple," Gideon replied. "You've got to stay in it one at a time, for as long as you can. The one who lasts longest is the winner."

While Gideon hadn't bothered with a costume, I noticed that he was wearing dark clothes: dark cord trousers, a dark hooded top, dark woollen gloves. No doubt he'd rigged the place up and would be creeping around, playing tricks. But this knowledge didn't make it easier. I could sense the light and warmth of the main house falling further and further behind us. When we reached the Spinney, and Gideon switched his torch on, it was even worse. The torchlight was a single blot dancing along the leaf-strewn path in front, intensifying the blackness around us; anything could be lurking there, and we wouldn't notice it. When we reached the Wendy House, the beam roved over its neglected façade, picking out the most repellent aspects: clumps of fungus, water stains that seemed to form ghastly faces.

He now gave us the rules in full. We had to draw straws to determine the order. Once that had been established, we must withdraw to the garage, and he'd bring us back in turn. There was a chair inside, and we had to sit in it. He would subsequently disappear – to where he didn't say, and the ordeal could begin. Once we'd fled the Wendy House, assuming we'd "survived", he would take us to wait in another place so that we couldn't return to the garage and tell the others what had happened.

There were squeaks of excitement combined with moans of very real fear.

"What if a fiend gets us?" Gary said.

"What if Red Clogs gets us?" Colin added.

"Stop farting around," Gideon replied. "I haven't got all night."

We went back to the garage, where we drew the straws. Sarah got the shortest, which meant that she had to go first. I suggested she stay in the garage and not participate, but she insisted she wanted to try. After her it was Gary, then Gaynor, then Pete, then me, then Dom, then Kevin, then Sally, then Colin.

Gideon led my sister away by the hand, and soon we were waiting by the garage door, listening intently. Not surprisingly given the distance, we heard very little. Gideon was back five minutes later, minus Sarah and looking pleased with himself. Gary gave the rest of us a haggard look before setting off into the darkness to take his own turn. When Gideon returned the second time, it was quicker than previously, and he looked even more pleased. Gaynor went next, and a short while later we thought we heard a faint scream. We stared at each other wide-eyed, the light of the jack-o-lanterns flickering on our ashen faces. No-one needed to say anything, but whatever was going to happen to us out there in the dark was surely not as bad as the waiting for it. It would soon be my turn, and I was physically trembling. With the sort of miscalculation only a rugby prop forward is capable of, Kevin tried to lighten the mood with a story about a pair of lads in America who'd disappeared but were later found stuffed with straw, their heads swapped around, and their legs stitched where their arms should be. The others aggressively shushed him – even Pete, who'd set out this evening with the apparent intent not to be impressed, but who now looked as scared as everyone else.

Pete was the next person up, but when Gideon arrived, he was no longer smiling – which was puzzling. From the speed of his return, Gaynor had lasted hardly any time at all, which I'd have thought would please him. Pete went off with shoulders hunched and fists clenched – his 'fighting posture'. Again however, Gideon was back in less than three minutes.

"Next?" he said from the drive. He'd never once come into the garage, but each time had stayed outside and summoned us in a sepulchral tone.

I saluted the ones left and went off with him. I'd expected it to be like a walk to the gallows, but to my surprise Gideon began to confide in me.

"Look Steve," he murmured. "You're one of the biggest here, so see if you can set the others an example, yeah? Try and last a bit longer. I spent two days on this, and it looks like it's all been for nothing."

"How long did the others last?" I asked.

"None more than two minutes. But you're going to show some bollocks, yeah? Make this worth my while."

Like I wasn't under enough pressure.

By the time we entered the Spinney, I was shivering. When I reached the Wendy House, I didn't dare look at it. He pulled its front door open and shone the torch inside. Everything in there was green with damp, except for the white plastic garden chair in the middle. There were other bits of furniture and lumber, but all were covered with stained sheets. It smelled like a stagnant pond, but I stepped inside anyway and sat down. He closed the door on me. It had a window at eye-level, minus glass. I gazed through it and watched as he retreated, switching his torch off so that he was nothing more than an amorphous blob weaving away though the thickets. Then he was gone.

If the waiting in the garage had been an ordeal, it was nothing compared to waiting alone in there. I was so tense that the slightest thing would have catapulted me from that seat. As such, it was amazing that I withstood the first challenge – when a pile of books suddenly cascaded from a high shelf in the corner, apparently of their own volition.

I leapt to my feet but didn't flee. My eyes had attuned to the gloom and, just before bolting, I'd caught a quick glimpse of a stick being withdrawn through a hole that had been drilled in the wall behind the books. This visual sign of trickery calmed my nerves a little, and I was able to withstand the second challenge. This involved a plastic teapot sliding along a fishing line pulled taut across the ceiling; I didn't see it at first, but felt the ice-cold water it was trickling, right down the back of my neck. Again, I almost ran, but before I could, I glanced up and spotted the apparatus. The third incident was more testing: the chair I was sitting on suddenly moved of its own accord, rolling and pitching. I even survived that, but when a hoarse voice began to whisper unintelligibly behind me, it was too much. Even though I guessed correctly that it was a tape recording, I ran.

I was half-way across the second lawn when Gideon popped up out of nowhere, again almost frightening me to death.

He grabbed me. "Okay, it's all right. Calm down."

"I couldn't," I stammered, "I just couldn't ..."

"At least you lasted longer than the others," he said, checking his watch. "Three and a half minutes to be precise. Follow me."

We set off back to the main house. As the garage was on the south side of it, we veered towards the north. But I was surprised when he opened a door in a small brick outbuilding. I'd never known this door be open before; Dom had only ever referred to it as "the washhouse". It was pitch black in there and freezing cold.

"What's this?" I said.

"Get in!" He shoved me from behind, banging the door closed.

"Gideon!" I shrieked.

And suddenly there were hands all over me, cold, rubbery hands touching my face, my hair. I squawked and spun around, desperately trying to find the door – only for the light of an electric torch to snap on, and howls of laughter to assail me. It was Sarah, Gary, Gaynor and Pete, all wearing washing-up gloves. This was where Gideon had made them wait while the rest of us went through our ordeal.

"Jesus," I said, "you scared the crap out of me."

I was promptly shushed by Gary, who switched the torch off and removed a cardboard sheet from in front of the small, cobweb-covered window. We peered out.

"Best laugh we've ever had this, I'll tell you," he whispered, oblivious to the exact same fun that had presumably been had at his own expense a few minutes earlier.

We watched in silence as the two shapes of Gideon and Dom trooped across the first lawn. Dom, already much smaller and weedier than his brother, was walking with the slouched posture of someone about to experience the worst thing in the world, which made him look even smaller. They vanished through the first holly hedge, and silence reigned – but not for long. Maybe as soon as a minute later, we heard cries of terror from the near distance. They grew in intensity, and then Dom reappeared through the hedge at full speed. He hared across the lawn, his Dracula cloak billowing behind him. Gideon came in hot pursuit, roaring at the top of his voice.

"You bloody little coward! Get back in!"

Dom spun around, protesting wildly. "Something fell over!"

"Get back in!" Gideon grabbed him by the scruff of his neck and marched him back through the gap in the holly hedge.

"But something fell over!"

"*Get back in!*" They vanished, but I could hear Gideon shouting all the way to the far end of the garden. "*Sarah bloody Carter lasted longer than you did!*"

We were in fits of giggles, which became uproarious laughter when we later learned that Gideon had thrown Dom back inside the Wendy House and locked the door, intent on subjecting him to the full gamut of special effects. Dom, ("rodent-like as ever," in Gideon's words), had eventually wriggled out through one of the windows and crept back by a different route, though ironically his brief incarceration put him in pole position. He lasted – if you could call it *lasting* – five full minutes. But even that was eventually bested. Sally lasted seven minutes, and Kevin lasted eight. I'm guessing that, having listened to the un-ghostlike hullabaloo in the garden during Dom's sojourn, they'd been able to put a face on the unknown, and it had reduced the fear factor. Surprisingly, the overall winner was

Colin, who made it ten whole minutes before fleeing for his life, though he hotly refuted Gideon's claims that he'd only managed it by sitting there with his eyes screwed shut and his hands clamped on his ears.

No-one ran the full gauntlet, so after the game Gideon took us back to the Wendy House, and, with his torch, showed us some of the things we'd have experienced if we'd been brave enough. These included a jack-in-the-box concealed under one of the sheets, which would have projected junk into the air, realistic animal grunts from the roof, and a ghastly figure lurching through the trees towards us with its head severed – this last one would have been pretty unnerving even though it would then have revealed itself to be Gideon, who *had* produced a costume after all, and a rather good one.

His mission accomplished, Gideon told us to grab some stuff for him when we went trick-or-treating and hurried off back to the house. His best mate Charlie Gulwick was due to call for him, and they were off to "a proper party". We wandered back to the garage, jabbering excitedly. Scream Inn had set the standard, and whatever game we played next it was going to need to be quality to maintain the mood. Which was when we noticed that we were missing one – Pete.

For no reason anyone could explain, he simply wasn't with us anymore.

At first, we assumed it was a joke, and we went to look for him warily, expecting that he'd jump growling from a bush. But that didn't happen.

Soon we began calling his name. Still there was no response.

"What shall we do?" Gary said.

"He was definitely in the washhouse with us?" I asked.

"Yeah, definitely."

Once again, the extensive grounds of the Blyford house became a benighted wilderness. During the course of the evening, we'd stopped sensing hostile presences in every shadow, and started seeing the place for what it was – a suburban garden that just happened to be a little larger and darker than most. That view was now reversed.

"No-one could have nabbed him when we went back to the Wendy House to have a look at Gideon's special effects, could they," Gaynor said. It was a statement, not a question. But she didn't sound convinced, and neither were the rest of us.

We went indoors to get help. Dom's older brother Clark came out. Clark was seventeen, and even taller and more handsome than Gideon. He was studying for his A-levels at the time, and very studious. Even on this occasion he wore gold-rimmed spectacles and was carrying a book. I suggested we tell Doctor Blyford, but Clark was having none of it. His father had just finished a long, hard day and was asleep in front of the television, so he couldn't be disturbed. From what I'd heard, Doctor Blyford spent most evenings asleep in front of the television regardless of whether he'd had a hard day or not. But I didn't argue. I was thirteen and Clark was seventeen, and in my eyes that made him God.

Clark put his denim jacket on and said he'd help us look. The search itself became a kind of game. Now that we had an older guy with us, we found the Dutch courage to venture far beyond the boundaries of the garden, even down into the Valley, which on Halloween night we were absolutely certain would be thronging with evil entities. At first, we searched along its upper slopes in a straggling, sniggering band. Clark gave us a few ghost stories of his own, all pinched from other sources though we didn't realise this at the time. He told us how a man, who'd been dared to spend the entire night alone in a haunted house was discovered in the morning with his hair turned white. He told us how an elderly lady had sat all evening in her armchair, reading a book and patting the dog beside her, only to then go to the bathroom and find the dog hanging from a wire noose – whose hairy head she'd been patting, she never found out.

These genuinely spooked us, but of course we had a seventeen-year-old with us, so we weren't totally scared. Besides, we were now getting annoyed. It was typical of the way Pete had been behaving recently for him to do something like this. Trick-or-treat was the most profitable part of the night, but this incident was eating into the time we'd allocated for it. We stopped half-way down the Valley, on the part of the slope overlooking Scubby Hollow. We called and called, but still there was no response.

"Do you think we should get the police?" Sally said.

Clark gave this some thought. "I think the best thing we can do is go back to the house and call his mother. See if he's gone home, yeah?"

We wandered back up the slope and wove towards Jubilee Crescent via the allotments and their sheds, still joking, still tittering, still playing spooky pranks on each other.

That was where we found him.

Kevin suddenly grabbed my arm. He pointed to a half-open shed door, through which two feet in training shoes were protruding.

"Nice one, Pete," I said. "Good joke, but thanks to you we're almost out of time."

Clark didn't see the funny side of it either. He broke away from us and sprinted over there. When he shone his torch inside, he grunted in shock. He tried to hold the rest of us back, but we were too many. We crammed the doorway and saw everything.

It was definitely Pete – we could tell that from his clown mask, which had been torn into quarters but then, bit by bit, had been placed back on his face like the pieces of a jigsaw puzzle. Thankfully this meant we couldn't see his head, which I later learned had been kicked like a football for several minutes. But his shirt had been torn off, so his chest and abdomen were clearly exposed. They'd been slashed every which way – back and forth, up and down, side to side. Lodged to the hilt at the point where his throat met his collarbone was a large pair of scissors.

8

Most of us didn't go back to school until after the memorial service held for Pete in St. Nathanial's Church a couple of days later. This was before the era of counselling. Child psychology was in its infancy. We'd had a shock, which was a shame, but we had to get over it because life went on. In those days, we weren't encouraged to cry for the television cameras or leave piles of flowers at the school gate. Grief was supposed to be a private thing rather than a form of public catharsis. Most likely we wouldn't remember much about it anyway – at least that was what the adults told each other. But just to be on the safe side, our parish priest, Father Carrickfergus, asked our mums and dads to keep us in the church after the service.

There's a lot of mythology aired about Catholic upbringings. There especially was back in the 1970s, when sectarianism still had persuasive power in places like Liverpool and Glasgow, never mind over in Northern Ireland. But that's all it was – mythology. The idea that we were educated in a strict, reproving atmosphere, tutored by humourless monks and nuns, who, if we didn't run around 'Hail Marying' all the time, or saying constant decades of the Rosary, would snap branches off the trees in order to scourge our heathen hides, and that as a result we'd grow up with complexes that we'd never get over for the rest of our lives – about sex being dirty, about drink being the devil in liquid form, about our souls being indelibly stained with mortal sins if we didn't go to church every Sunday – all of that was bollocks. I had a perfectly happy, normal upbringing as a Catholic child. It was robust certainly, as Mr. Lord – who was neither a monk nor even a Catholic – exemplified. But things were tougher for everyone back then; youth discipline had not yet become an unfashionable concept, and you won't need me to tell you that we had a better society because of it.

Anyway, as I was saying, Father Carrickfergus asked us – just the ones who'd been present at the scene of the murder – to wait in the church after the service. We had our parents with us and sat quietly in the pews, while he strode up and down the central aisle. Despite the mournful occasion, a couple of us – though not me, I'd been too close to Pete – had trouble keeping straight faces. He was a tall, painfully thin chap, Father Carrickfergus, with a 'feather-duster' mop of white hair, and only one hand; the other hand was a ridiculously small glove, which was permanently clenched into a fist. We used to call him 'Stump', not realising at the time that he'd lost that hand as a trainee priest in a seminary in France, when the Gestapo had chopped it off with an axe because he'd refused to reveal the hiding places of Jewish fugitives.

"Trust me when I tell you this, children," he said in a strained voice. "I too have experienced a reign of darkness. I too have been face-to-face with pure, unnatural evil."

Pure, unnatural evil. The memory of those *clinking* footfalls in the fog came back to haunt me, and I felt as if I was going to pee my pants.

"But I promise you it cannot last," he added. "A time will come when the darkness has passed, because it always does, and always will. Meanwhile, you may wonder why God, in His infinite wisdom and mercy, would allow such a thing into this world in the first place. All I can say is that it's a mystery that will not be resolved for us until our final day. But I promise you children that nothing in God's creation exists without having a purpose. Everything happens for a reason – as part of His grand design. Even the most malevolent things will lead ultimately to a greater good. Remember that, children, and never despair."

Malevolent things. My thoughts lingered on Pete's face, thankfully hidden behind his torn, bloodstained clown mask.

"'I am with you always,' Jesus said," Father Carrickfergus told us. "'To the end of time.' And he won't go back on that promise. He is always here, walking alongside us. I make you a solemn vow that, even in times of trial like this, the most terrible forces of darkness will never put out the light of God's love."

I suppose to some it would have been inspirational. But to me it was baffling. How could the forces of darkness have any other purpose than to be destroyed? What was God playing at allowing them to exist? But how did you go about destroying a demonic being anyway? I remembered Gaynor's recitation of *The Exorcist* story. They'd destroyed that monster, or at least dispatched it back to Hell by reading prayers to it, yet according to what Gaynor's sister had said, at least two priests had died in the process. And supposedly it was a true story – which wasn't very encouraging.

Some of us may have left that meeting in the church feeling better. Others may have left just glad it was over. I'm not sure what I thought, but I was vaguely hopeful that if God was still in control of things – and it was a big 'if' after the events of the last few days – it would probably work out in the end. The thought of Jesus walking alongside me was reassuring, but I'd have preferred it if I could see and hear him.

9

The general feeling was that Pete had finally got tired of playing second-fiddle to Dom and his family and had sneaked off on his own – either to punish us by spoiling the party, or because he was bored and going home. It was assumed he'd climbed over the garden's rear fence so that no-one would spot him and had met his killer while crossing the allotments.

We refused to consider the horrifying possibility that the killer might have been in the garden with us all along, just waiting his chance. The police dismissed that idea too – and they discussed it with each one of us in detail; they said it was inconceivable that a careful predator like this would have taken such a risk. Yet the more we youngsters thought about it, the more we reminded ourselves that this was no ordinary predator.

We called our council of war for the day after we returned to lessons – at least, *some* of us did. It was a Friday, and I'd arranged to meet Dom and Gary in the school library at lunchtime, but only Dom showed up. It's strange the effect something like this can have, not just on you but on those around you. I later discovered that Gary had been told by his mother not to associate with the rest of us anymore, as if it was somehow our fault that he'd nearly been murdered. Gary being Gary, he was red-faced and apologetic, but he said that his

71

mother was serious, and trust me, when Gary's mother was *serious*, she wasn't someone you wanted to get on the wrong side of.

But there was also a feeling of hostility towards us from other kids. This was because, as a mark of respect to Pete and his family (and presumably because there was now a costly security element to consider), the school's annual bonfire party was cancelled. Even on our first day back, when we were all still in a state of shock, there were scowls directed at us from some of the older pupils. One tried to trip me on the stairs, after making loud comments about "brainless pillocks who let their friends die, and now the rest of us have to pay for it". Even my own parents behaved strangely. My father sat me down for a "man to man chat". To my initial bewilderment, this was all about the birds and the bees, though he later tried to tie it in with current events by saying that he thought sex was almost certainly the reason for the two murders. In a self-contradiction bordering on the irrational, he then asked me sternly if we'd done anything to offend anyone, if we owed anyone money, and if we'd been getting involved with gangs. This typically confused adult thinking gave me even more reason not to voice my suspicions to my parents or even to the police – not until I'd discussed it with my pals.

"They wouldn't believe it anyway," Dom said. We were now in the library, at a table concealed behind several tall racks of books. "I'm not sure *I* believe it, if I'm honest."

"But I'm telling you, I heard those clog-irons in the fog," I replied. "They clattered after me all along Mulberry Road."

"Surely there's no such thing as Red Clogs?"

"That's what we're here to find out." I'd selected a load of books from the nearby shelves, all of which I expected to be mines of information on the ghosts and spirits of Northern England.

"We'll never get through all these," Dom complained.

"When Gary arrives, he can help us."

But of course, Gary didn't arrive. We watched the clock for a few minutes, before giving up and commencing to read. This in itself became an atmospheric experience. It was only lunchtime, but already dark and cold outside, and lashing with November rain. The library was located in the oldest wing of the school and was made almost entirely of bare stone and wood panelling. It was gloomy at the best of times, but now multiple shadows trickled down its tall stained-glass windows, reflecting over us in liquid patterns as we flipped page after sinister page. I discovered horrors that I'd never imagined. From *Lancashire Legends*, I learned about the Pendle Witches, the Cromwellian spectres of Chingle Hall and 'Jenny Greenteeth', a vile hag who swam the rivers of the Northwest, seeking to lure children to watery graves. In *Northern Spooks*, I read about the 'barguest' or 'hill-ghost', a half-man-half-animal thing, which roamed the highest and bleakest moors; the mere sight of it was a promise of impending doom.

But it was Dom who discovered the *crème de la crème*.

"Oh my God," he said in a low, stunned voice. "Listen to this." He began to read: "'A supernatural being of evil intent. A dark spirit of the underworld once believed capable of walking on the Earth and causing mayhem. Much feared during Anglo-Saxon times, its origins lie in Norse or Germanic myth. Many stories tell how this shapeless boggle would assume human proportion and bestride the night, brutally killing anyone it encountered.'"

My jaw had virtually dropped, but it was to drop even further. "What is it?"

Dom fixed me with a bug-eyed stare that would have done justice to Colin Lapwing. "According to this, it's called an 'ettin'."

"An ettin?" I'd been expecting something a bit more dramatic. But then it hit me. "Bloody hell … Ettinshall Colliery!

Dom nodded. "Remember when we were told in History how place-names give clues to events that happened in the past?"

"Ettin's Hall!" I said again, loving the sound as it slid from my tongue. "Maybe this thing's always lived up there? Hang on … Red Clogs was a pitman who got killed. It's a ghost, not some monster from the underworld."

"Yeah but that pitman was killed underground, wasn't he? Maybe the two sort of mixed together?" Dom's eyes widened even more, as if he'd amazed himself with such an original line of thought. "Maybe that's how Red Clogs came to

74

be? You know, one helped the other. I mean, ordinary dead people don't come back, do they?"

"Some do."

"Steve, it's *got* to have something to do with it."

I nodded solemnly.

Shock, fear, plus the sensational nature of recent events had served as a catalyst. It was now fixed firmly in our minds that Ettinshall was the colliery where the Red Clogs of my grandad's mythmaking hung out, even though my grandad had never mentioned the colliery by name. Despite one of the victims being our best friend, for which reason you may think we ought to have treated the subject more reverently, we now knew for an indisputable fact that Red Clogs was the culprit.

"I am *sooo* glad Bommy Night has been cancelled," I said. "There's no way I'm going out after dark now."

I glanced again at *Lancashire Legends* and *Northern Spooks*; their illustrations were done as crude, heavily inked line drawings, a style very popular in children's books of that era. Somehow, this rendered them even more diabolical. The Pendle witches were grotesque, with stunted bodies, warty noses and hands like eagles' claws; the barguest was even more terrifying – a formless thing of hair, fangs and blazing eyes. I pushed both books away from me as if they were tainted.

"Well, listen, here's the thing," Dom said, beckoning.

I leaned over the table.

"It's probably for the best that the others aren't here," he whispered. "Because, if you're interested, Bommy Night's not been cancelled – not totally. Clark says that, while the school bommy's off, we can have one in our back garden. Just a small one, with close friends and family. You're invited as long as you don't mention it to anyone."

"Hmmm." I pondered – for about three seconds. "Okay, I'll be there."

Pete's death had obviously been a tragedy, but deep down most of us reckoned that cancelling November 5th had been a bit of an overreaction. How else were we supposed to "get over it" if we weren't allowed to have some fun?

10

As it turned out, Dom's small bonfire party was not going to be small at all, and I soon got the feeling that it had been on the cards since before the school party had been cancelled. Clark Blyford maintained the fiction that he was organising it as a minor consolation for "the kids affected by the loss of their mate". But Dom and I were the only kids invited who'd actually experienced this sad event, while the majority of those coming would be Clark's friends.

Nevertheless, Bonfire Night preparations quickly came to dominate our thinking. The bonfire was to be built on the first lawn, and Dom and I were charged with making the Guy Fawkes. We got to this with great enthusiasm that very first night, going through both our respective wardrobes to produce an old pair of black trousers and a dark, ragged coat. We fastened these constituent parts together by punching holes in them and looping string through, and then scavenged all around the garden for dry leaves that we could stuff them with.

Gideon appeared, as he always seemed to when something vaguely interesting was going on, and told us that our Guy was pathetic as it didn't have hands, feet or a head. We shared this view to an extent. For the head, we'd planned to fill a bag with screwed-up newspaper and attach it to the shoulders by fastening it to a stick, which we would shove down through the neck, but the hands and feet would be more problematic. We eventually resolved this by digging out an old pair of work boots from the Blyfords' under-stair closet, while my Mum volunteered some driving gloves, which she'd bought for my Dad on his previous birthday, only for him to loftily declare that he needed full skin-contact with the steering wheel if he wanted to avoid the sort of accidents that women drivers routinely had. We were pleased with the final result and stored it safely in the garage. Gideon came and checked it out, and this time said that it was okay. The job he'd been given was to build the bonfire itself, but if there was one thing Gideon was really good at, it was delegating.

"You two can give me a hand now you've finished with the Guy. I'm really busy at present. Why don't you collect some firewood?"

Eager beavers, we hastened to comply. Unfortunately, there wasn't much firewood lying around the garden. We tried snapping a few twigs off trees, only for Gideon to come outside again, a Sven Hassel novel in his hand, and rebuke us – firstly for vandalising the garden, and secondly for being such dunces that we thought fresh wood, full of sap, would burn. When we pointed out that we couldn't find any firewood, he ordered us to improvise.

The normal thing at this time of year would be to 'raid bommies'. Health and Safety regulations were still far in the future in 1974, so everywhere you went in our borough in early November, you'd see bonfires standing on waste-ground. These weren't just constructed from timber, but also tyres, boxes, anything that would ignite. They were a prime source of material if you yourself were short, though you had to be careful. I knew several lads who'd been caught raiding other kids' bommies and had been leathered for their trouble. On this occasion it would be even riskier. For one thing, there were fewer bommies to choose from – the recent murders meant that only half the normal number of youngsters would be allowed out after dark (even the tireless penny-for-the-Guy gangs were absent once night fell). This curfew extended to us as well: I was only allowed out after dark if I was going to Dom's, and Dom was only allowed out if he was going to mine. It meant that if we were to go raiding, we'd have to do it during the day, which increased exponentially our chances of getting caught.

It was Charlie Gulwick who suggested an alternative. Charlie was Gideon's best pal, and a short, chunky chap with spiky yellow hair and grinning, chimp-like features. I'd never really trusted him; I found him a sly presence, but a lot of the time, like Gideon, he could be tolerable, even enjoyable company.

"There's stacks of firewood up at Ettinshall," he said, when he arrived later that evening. "I was up there last week. There's mountains of the stuff next to the washery."

"There you go," Gideon said to us, pleased that the whole thing was sorted. "Take the wheelbarrow."

Dom and I exchanged disbelieving stares.

"I'm not going up *there*," Dom said. "Not in the dark."

"Go tomorrow afternoon. There's nothing to worry about, there're loads of people there during the day … dog-walkers, motorbike-scramblers."

"Tramps," Charlie added, sniggering.

"Are there heck tramps!" Gideon snapped, mouthing at him to shut up – recent rumours were doing the rounds that the murderer was a tramp, though of course we youngsters knew better. "Take the wheelbarrow, lads. Get as much as you can."

The next day was a Saturday, so we didn't really have an excuse not to go. But the mere thought of venturing up to Ettinshall made us shudder. Perhaps sensing this, Gideon was nicer than normal to us for the rest of that night. He and Charlie had intended to spend it prowling the streets, throwing lit bangers into gardens. He let us join in, and it proved to be so much fun that we soon forgot everything else. We even forgot that we weren't supposed to leave the boundaries of Dom's property. But when I got home later that night and hit the sack, I remembered the ordeal that was facing me the next day, and sleep proved elusive.

11

The mellow conditions of early autumn were now dwindling in November's wintry blast. The next few weeks would see pelting rain and hail and at night, when it was clear, there'd be frost and ice. October's red-gold brocade would soon hang in dismal, skeletal shreds. That Saturday was the true beginning of this.

I called at Dom's house just after lunchtime; the afternoon was lit by a dull, milk-grey light blurred around its edges by a Northwest English phenomenon that we called 'Manchester mist' – a light, bitterly cold drizzle so fine that it hung in the saturated air like steam. I had my trusty Parka on, but, for the first time since March, I was wearing gloves too. Dom came out similarly attired and together we dragged the wheelbarrow from the garage.

"I still think this is a crap idea," I said, my breath pluming.

He shrugged as if he agreed with me but, Gideon having issued the order, was helpless to do otherwise.

"Any firewood will be soaked," I added.

"We've still got to get it. If we collect it today and put it under cover it'll have dried out by the 5th. Anyway, Gideon said we'll put petrol on it if it won't burn."

"Someone should put petrol on Gideon. Where's *he* gone while we're doing all the hard work?"

"Went to town this morning with Charlie. They're buying the fireworks."

I groaned at having missed out on such a treat. As preparations for Bonfire Night went, there was little to touch the joy of roving excitedly from shop to shop, gazing at rows of rockets, Catherine-Wheels, Traffic Lights and Roman Candles. Even if the alternative hadn't been traipsing alone up to the bleak no man's land that was Ettinshall Colliery, I would have got a real kick out of that.

Dom pocketed a gun-shaped cigarette lighter, which he'd filched from Clark's room in case we needed to look through any of the old colliery buildings, then ravelled up a length of washing-line, chucked it in the barrow, and we walked down Jubilee Crescent towards the top of the Valley. We made sure to give the allotments wide berth, though we wouldn't have been allowed to walk through them anyway as they were still cordoned off with police tape. A police mobile incident-room – in those days a battered old caravan – was also parked there. We stared at it as we set off down the slope, and continued staring as it receded behind us. There were no officers around, but it served as a clear reminder that what we were doing here was kind of stupid.

I think I've mentioned before how dreary Scubby Hollow could be in late autumn. Once down there, the trees were twisted stanchions almost completely denuded of foliage. Our feet

82

squelched in mud and heaps of trampled leaves. The wheelbarrow became steadily more difficult to manage, its single rusty wheel ploughing a deep furrow. Even Hill Bank Close, when we finally got down to it, was no improvement. At this low point, it was unmade and churned into quagmires. The woods to either side of it were black and dripping. You wouldn't have recognised the sun-dappled glades where we'd spent the summer. And of course, the Manchester Mist was now mingling with real mist from the river, making a foggy backdrop on the far edge of our vision. As we crossed the bridge, all we could hear was the squeaking of the wheelbarrow and the occasional splash as unseen objects dropped into the Redwater. On the other side, the path rose uphill again, away from the miasma of the lower Valley and onto firmer ground. This was a bit of a relief, especially when we crossed the railway bridge and joined the stony track that led to the farm.

"There's nothing to worry about," Dom said with forced cheerfulness. "It's daylight. He doesn't walk in daylight, remember."

I nodded in agreement but took no real comfort. As daylight went, this was a poor example – it might as well have been shining through a dingy pane; but it wasn't just that. Dom had finally given voice to the fear we both harboured and thus far hadn't mentioned. Rather than relieve the tension, it felt more as if he'd issued an open challenge.

The farmhouse and its outbuildings were like something from medieval history, built from rough, basic stones, with roofs of sagging, moss-eaten slates. There was nobody around. A black dog lay in the entrance to the stable. This was the main reason we hadn't brought Sheba with us – the farm-dog was supposedly a "bad 'un". Its ears twitched and it watched us intently as we passed, but it didn't run out to meet us, or even bark.

It knows where we're going, I remember thinking. *The mere thought scares it.*

As we moved on from the farm into a flat, misty hinterland, I felt as if we were leaving the last outpost of civilisation.

"It could also be," Dom added in a conversational tone, which didn't fool me at all, "that Ettinshall isn't actually where Red Clogs is supposed to come from. We don't know where it happened for sure."

On one hand he may have been right – there'd been countless collieries in Ashburn. In my parents' youth, its sooty landscape had sprouted pitheads and factory chimneys as if its life depended on them (which it basically had done). But the murders had happened *here* – in this particular corner of town, where Ettinshall was located. Denying this truth out loud would serve no purpose, because it wouldn't change it.

Gradually, the farmland gave way to cindery waste. The gutted shells of freestanding buildings appeared, broken ruins whose purpose was long forgotten. Any vegetation was rank scrub-brush; the rich soil of the lower slopes had turned to barren clinker. To one side of the track, we saw a burned-out car. Gangs of troublesome kids would sometimes drive up here to dump their stolen motors. There was nothing new in that even back in 1974, but it was less heartening that no-one had ever retrieved the charred wreck – how long had it been here, and yet nothing had been done to dispose of it? Maybe no-one in authority even knew about it.

We were now on the colliery brow. No trees grew here, and there was minimal undergrowth. Buildings closed in, all either filled with the stinking rubbish of long disuse or boarded up with planks and strips of corrugated metal. We entered the main concourse, which faced onto the vandalised frontages of the winding-house and the pithead offices. The brick edifice of the pithead tower loomed over us, though only girders remained of its top half, and its colossal flywheels had long been removed. Its various entrances had been closed up with iron grilles, though most of these were rusted and slashed with spray-paint.

For some reason, it was a little less frightening now that we were actually here.

We left the wheelbarrow and began to explore. We both had a vague idea where the washery was. But to get there we had to go through what had once been called the 'screens'. Again, this was a hollow shell, its complex mechanised guts long ago ripped out. Our footsteps echoed as we walked through the cavernous spaces beneath its hangar-like awnings. Shredded cables hung down, steel bolts jutted up. Of the sorting engines, the rollers, the tippers and the massive conveyor-belts that had once brought up great glistening heaps of virgin coal, there was no longer a trace. At the back of this was a high, hooded structure that we'd always referred to as 'the coal elevator'. At the time I had no idea what this was. It was several stories high, but flimsy and rotted through, its beams showing rib-like between tatters of tarpaper. Underneath the coal elevator, there was a siding from where a mineral line had formerly dispatched rubble to the far-off humps of the slag heaps, but this siding was now filled with bricks, and the mineral line was nothing but a flattened track meandering into a smoggy distance. About twenty yards along it, stood the washery tower – distinct for its upside-down funnel shape – and right next to this, as Charlie had promised, there was a mountainous pile of loose timber.

Dom whooped as he ran forward. I have to admit, I was pleased too.

As soon as we'd arrived, we'd seen stray bits of wood all over the brow, so we could have collected sufficient eventually if we'd been prepared to wander about, but here was our one-stop-shop. It was damp, but not drenched. To this day I'm not sure who'd heaped it there, or why, but it was just what we wanted: planks, staves and props, all broken up into manageable lengths.

"I'll get the barrow," I said, running back beneath the elevator and through the screens to the concourse.

I grabbed the barrow by the handles and glanced around once before trundling off. With decayed ruins on all sides, it was easy to imagine you were being watched, but just for the moment

I was happy that we'd found what we'd come here for.

For the next hour or so, Dom and I loaded wood onto our vehicle; in fact, we loaded far more than we could realistically transport. Dom had his length of washing-line, with which we intended to strap it all in place, but we soon had so much wood that the line wasn't long enough. We weren't deterred. We threw it all off again, and went for quality rather than quantity, selecting only the driest, sturdiest pieces, which was a time-consuming process. Our cheerful laughs rang across the derelict site, echoing through its empty buildings and passages. Two hours had soon gone, during which we were completely oblivious to the gradual darkening of the sky.

It took a sudden sound of metal banging on metal to bring us to our senses.

We both looked up at the same time.

The sound had only lasted a few seconds and then stopped. We listened for it again but heard nothing. Only now did we notice how much colder and gloomier it was. The drizzle had ceased, and the air temperature was almost freezing; daylight had faded, to be replaced by that deep blue dimness of dusk. The banging sound might have come from a shutter tapping in the breeze, but it hadn't sounded like that to me. It had been steady and repeated, as if someone was making it deliberately.

I suggested it was time to go, and Dom agreed. Again, we tried to loop the washing-line around our pile of firewood, but we still had too much.

The two ends of the line wouldn't even meet. We threw a few more pieces off, and at last managed to tie a knot, though it wasn't very secure. More firewood would slip loose. We didn't care. We manoeuvred the barrow around so that it was facing the elevator and, beyond that, the screens, and started forward. It was much more difficult now with so heavy a load.

"It'll be nothing," Dom said airily. "There're all kinds of strange noises round here."

"Strange noises round here," a voice repeated.

We halted in our tracks.

"Was that an echo?" I said. But if it had been, my own words didn't echo.

We gazed through the screens. It was chasmal, black with oil and dirt. There were numerous apertures leading out; doors, windows. At the far end, there was a double-sized entrance, though all we could see beyond that was the deepening dusk. Nothing moved, yet I could have sworn that the voice had come from somewhere ahead of us.

"Let's go another way," I said.

"Another way," the voice repeated, and this time it had definitely *not* been an echo. I knew my own voice, and this wasn't it. This voice was oddly high-pitched, almost shrill.

We began to backtrack. I'm not sure at which point we abandoned the wheelbarrow and ran. We weren't even sure which direction we were headed in. Any would have done at that moment, but unfortunately, we ran down a blind alley – between two rows of old maintenance sheds. The only escape was at the far end, where there was a brick wall with an iron gate hanging open. We were half-way towards it, when the gate slammed closed. Even now, so many years later, that moment is impressed in my memory: the gate swinging closed with extreme force, as though to a strong but invisible hand.

It was a measure of how frightened we were that we didn't stop to discuss this, but instinctively veered left, crashing into one of the sheds. It was awful in there, dark and filthy, its roof having collapsed, its floor cluttered with all manner of rot and foulness. There was no other exit, so we climbed – like monkeys, swinging up through the rafters and jags of corrugated metal. We slashed our hands and tore our clothes, but it didn't bother us. We leapt down on the other side, but still found no respite. We were in a second narrow passage, with another gaunt ruin standing in front of us. To go left would take us back towards the screens; to go right would take us down to the far end of the maintenance sheds, close by that iron gate again. The decision was made for us when we heard a bang in the shed to our rear. We hared across the passage, straight through the arched door into the next building.

Built from solid brick, this place was more intact than others on the brow, but a sickening smell of damp pervaded its interior. We hastened up a central passage, the floor of which appeared to be tiled. As most of these were cracked and covered with greasy mould, we both slipped and fell at least once. To either side were what appeared to be wooden stalls with benches in them. At the far end was a T-junction, lit by a broken skylight through which water dripped.

Gasping for breath, we glanced behind us – the entrance to the building was a pale rectangle. At any second, we expected something horrible to appear there.

"Which way?" Dom panted.

I led him left into another tiled passage, wider than the previous one but much darker. Dom dug Clark's lighter out and flicked it on. In its dull, small glow, we saw rusted showerheads fitted at regular intervals. Clearly, we were in the old pit-baths. In which case there ought to be a back entrance or fire escape. I forged ahead, Dom following. At the end of the shower corridor, there was a wide stone-flagged area. The glow of the lighter revealed four cast-iron bathtubs. All were heavily corroded; the wall behind them had rotted away in lumps, revealing a mass of pipework.

We heard a scraping sound from somewhere behind us – in the entry passage. Another scraping sound followed. And another. I imagined metal soles on the tiled floor.

"Oh shit," Dom breathed, clicking his flame off.

We retreated, our eyes fixed on the shower corridor. Beyond the bathtubs, a curtain of old polythene, opaque with greenish grime, hung from one side of the room to the other. We backtracked towards it, hardly daring to breathe, but when we passed through it our feet clattered on shards of porcelain. We frantically shushed each other, and then, sensing that we might not be alone, glanced around. In a shaft of luminescence courtesy of another skylight, we saw the shells of four commodes. There were jagged holes in the walls and floor where they'd once been attached.

But that wasn't the main thing.

The main thing was standing just to the left of us.

Slowly, with skin crawling, we turned to look.

It was ragged and man-shaped, and at first, I thought it was tall, taller than any normal man had a right to be. Then I realised that it wasn't tall, but hovering – about two feet from the ground. In consequence, its head was so far up that it was lost in the gloom. But down below, its floating feet were clearly visible. They were enormous and clad in heavy boots, which, even in this dimness, we could see were caked in a thick, red substance.

I gave a choked squeal. Dom's hand spasmed open, his lighter crashing to the floor.

When we ran this time, we ran without knowing it.

We exited the bathhouse via its rear door, which we seemed to find instinctively. The next thing, we were going pell-mell over masses of slag and rubble, shouting hoarsely. The ground began to slope downward, which hopefully meant we were descending into the Valley, though there was a still a dreadfully long way to go. I risked a backward glance. Dom, less of an athlete than me, was about twenty yards behind, the eyes bulging in his white face. I can't be certain, but I thought a gangling shape was close at his rear. This goaded me to near superhuman efforts, and Dom too. We vaulted the first barbed wire fence as if it wasn't there. After that, we were running on pasture rather than clinker, but we didn't slow down. We vaulted another fence, and another. A bunch of heifers scattered as we charged through them. Now we were running downhill. The next obstacle was a low wall, on the other side of which we slid on our backsides down a steep embankment, ripping through bracken and thorns, before alighting on the track-bed of the old branch line. I glimpsed the stone arch of the railway bridge about forty yards to our right. That was the obvious way to go – that was the path leading to the footbridge over the river. But all that mattered now was to keep going, to put as much distance between ourselves and Ettinshall as we possibly could, and the best thing for that was a straight line, right? We thus scrambled up the next embankment and raced down another sloping meadow, at the end of which we had to negotiate a higher, more complex barbed wire fence. Dom tried to climb through it rather than over it and got tangled. Normally he'd have hung there, bleating for help. On this occasion he fought his way through, though it left deep lacerations in his hands and arms.

At last we were descending through trees. Mist rose around us; the tang of humus filled the air. When we hit the Valley bottom, we struggled forward through deep sedge, knowing we'd shortly come to that most impassable barrier of all, the Redwater. It was now so dark that, when we reached the river, I almost fell in; only Dom's desperate hand clutching the hood of my Parka prevented it. We roamed in an easterly direction, weaving through increasingly dense hawthorn. It was crazy. The only way to get across the Redwater from here was via the Scubby Hollow footbridge, but I didn't want to go back that way. I feared that whatever had been pursuing us would be waiting for us there. And yet it was insane to continue blindly in the other direction.

Eventually I brought us to a halt. "We've got to think sensibly. We'll never get over at this rate."

"A tree leaning across the river," Dom gasped. "A low branch …"

I shook my head. "You know what the river's like at this time of year. Look how deep it's running, look how fast it is. If we fall in, we've no chance."

We could both swim and in our first instant of panicked flight I'd half entertained the idea that, if all else failed, I could breaststroke my way to the other shore. But now that I was actually facing the Redwater, gliding silt-black and silent between its steep, wooded banks, I had second thoughts.

A snapping twig jerked us into frantic flight again.

We heard this from the undergrowth somewhere ahead, so now, whether we liked it or not, we were headed back towards Scubby Hollow – only for a tall figure to emerge from the murk directly in front of us. Our shrieks were so loud and piercing that wood pigeons scattered from the branches overhead.

"What the hell are you lunatics playing at?" Gideon said, looking thoroughly startled.

On realising it was him, we collapsed to our knees, shoulders heaving, tears mingling with the sweat on our cheeks. At first, we couldn't speak. Another figure emerged from the trees behind us. We almost jumped again, but it was only Charlie.

"What're you … what're you doing here?" I finally stammered.

"Looking for you two," Gideon said. "You've been ages."

"No, what're you doing down *here*!"

"We saw you from the railway bridge. Running like the bloody clappers. We followed you, but you were running so fast it took us this long to catch up with you."

Now that he mentioned it, they too were flushed and wild-eyed.

"It was Red Clogs," Dom said, breathless.

Gideon gave him a long, dubious stare. We tried to explain what had happened – in fractured, unintelligible sentences. Gideon would later describe us as "gibbering girlishly". At first, he and Charlie were amused, apparently on the verge of laughing hysterically. But the more we told them, the more irritable Gideon became.

"So, where's the firewood?" he demanded. "Are you dumb clucks saying you left it behind?"

"Gideon, we didn't just make this up," Dom protested. "We *saw* Red Clogs!"

"You *thought* you saw him."

"It was in the pit-baths," I said. "If you don't believe us, go and check."

"Don't worry, we will. And we'll get the firewood while we're at it. And don't think I won't tell everyone about this latest display of cowardice, Dominic. And as for you, Steve – call yourself a rugby player? All I can say is that you're diminished in my eyes." He and Charlie stalked off up the slope. "That's what happens when you leave kids to do a man's job," I heard Gideon say.

Dom wanted to go after them and stop them – Gideon was his brother after all, and he was concerned for his safety. But I grabbed him and made him stay where he was.

"Let 'em go," I said. "Let 'em find out the truth for themselves, whatever the truth is."

As I've already mentioned, Gideon could be all right in small doses, but there were many flaws in his character. I wouldn't have specifically called him a bully, but he always had to be top dog and, with youngsters like us, that was easier for him. When Charlie arrived, the transformation was complete. Individually they were bearable, but when they came together, they could be two halves of a completely different whole – scornful, arrogant, full of cocky bravado. He still had Dom in his thrall, but I was getting tired of it.

With no other option, we walked west along the river until we came to the Scubby Hollow footbridge. We crossed this and strode nervously up Hill Bank Close. The dank blackness of the wood was a cloying presence, but we hurried up the track without looking left or right, and at last reached its street-lit upper section where the houses were.

12

We knew what we'd seen. There was no doubt in our minds, and the fun and frolics of Bonfire Night could not distract from it. Yet it's a mark of our volatile modern age that even the very strange can quickly be superseded by the completely mundane – even for someone like me, who'd now experienced the strange at first hand.

Like the Halloween party, the bonfire party started out well enough.

To both Dom's and my surprise, Gideon had returned later that Saturday evening with the wheelbarrow and firewood and stashed it all in the garage. When Dom asked him what had happened, Gideon's pugnacious response had been that nothing at all had happened, except that Bonfire Night had been saved, no thanks to we two "dickheads, who couldn't organise a wank in a warm bath". But he was right about one thing – Bonfire Night had been saved. By the morning of November 5th, Gideon and Clark had constructed a combustible pyramid in the corner of the Blyford house's first and largest lawn, which reached maybe eight feet in height.

I arrived there at just around seven o'clock that evening. I didn't have any fireworks – my Dad mistrusted them so much that he'd only given me permission to attend so long as I solemnly promised that only Dom's father and older brothers would be handling them – but my Mum gave me a tray of toffee apples that she'd made herself. The party was already under way; the fire ablaze, the Guy propped up in a chair on the very top of it. The neighbourhood echoed with what sounded like gunfire, the sky bursting with multi-coloured lights. As I entered the garden through the back door of the house, I saw Clark skipping backward across the grass, having just lit a row of three rockets, all of which soared upward in unison, detonating overhead in spectacular showers of sparks.

Quite a few people were in attendance whom I didn't know. There were several denim-clad hippy types – presumably Clark's college mates. There were also a couple of neighbours, and a thin bespectacled woman with two well-groomed children. I later learned that this was Dom's Aunt Clara and her offspring, James and Juliet, who'd come all the way down from Cumbria on a visit. Even Doctor Blyford appeared for a brief time, wearing his usual heavy overcoat and gloves, and smiling and nodding to all and sundry, but not speaking much. Beth was there too, which made me feel all warm and fuzzy. She wasn't staying for the whole evening, but while she was present, she'd be operating the food table. This was set out on the patio, and groaning beneath a weight of Bonfire Night treats, which included baked potatoes wrapped in foil, Lancashire hot-pot, black peas, parkin cake, trays of blackjacks and a bowl of soft, homemade treacle. When I offered my toffee apples, she thanked me profusely and set them in a place of honour in the very middle.

Unfortunately, her boyfriend was also present. This was the first time I'd met him. Remember how I explained that in the early 1970s boys of our age all tended to be called Paul, Peter, John or Stephen? Well, boys of a slightly older age – i.e. late teens – all tended to be called Mick or Tony or Baz. This one was definitely a Mick. In fact, his full name, Mick Stone, was highly appropriate, the monosyllables of both those monikers implying, to me at least, a gruff, brutish nature. He was very much a child of that era. He rode a motorbike and wore the appropriate fringed leather jacket. He had longish, black hair and thick, black sideburns. There was something of Mick Jagger about him, except that he wasn't thin or effeminate – quite the opposite; he was brawny and mean looking. I couldn't imagine what Beth saw in him, though I suppose it was that tiresome 'bad boy' thing, which male rebels of every new decade behave as if they've invented.

Compared to Mick Stone, even Charlie was a friendly face. He showed up about half an hour later with a tin box so large that he needed to carry it in both hands. When we opened it, it was packed with fireworks – which Dom, Gideon and I thought was seriously cool, even though we already had a stockpile. Most guests had contributed a few. Doctor Blyford had been particularly generous, providing three large boxes of Standard Fireworks, which were the kind of Government-approved ones. But Charlie's batch was the icing on the cake – it contained several ultra-large 'display' fireworks, and meant we'd be lighting up the garden and blowing up the sky for the next two hours at least.

And that's basically what happened.

The acrid smell of gunpowder soon hung everywhere. Our faces were seared by the heat and glare of the bonfire, which burned with increasing height and ferocity whenever Clark piled more wood onto it, quickly reducing the Guy Fawkes to ashes, and bringing delighted cheers from the crowd as two Jumping Jacks, which Gideon had concealed inside its head, went bouncing all over the place. As well as the Roman Candles, Olympic Flames, Old Volcanoes and Feathered Serpents, we had Little Demons, Snowstorms, Crystal Cascades. We even had the infamous Aeroplane, the firework with wings, which would never pass safety standards today because it was designed to be thrown through the air. And there was no end to the rockets, which raced upward all night, creating kaleidoscopic blood-red or aqua-green supernovas.

Of course, Bonfire Night being what it was, disaster was always close at hand. I think it was the previous year, 1973, when the National Health Service in the United Kingdom reported treating over three-thousand serious firework-related injuries. Mainly this was because people got too excited at bonfire parties and threw caution to the wind. There was also the 'bored adult' factor. Grown-ups find fireworks tedious. They can put up with them for the first half hour, before the warmth of the indoors and the promise of a few drinks become preferable. Thus, hordes of giddy youngsters are left in charge of items that are basically miniature explosives. However, when things went wrong at our party, it was not because of negligence or reckless behaviour – it was because of Red Clogs.

At least, that was what Dom afterwards insisted it was.

It was mid-evening and he was standing very close to the fire. It was dying down a little by now, and a few of us had seized the opportunity to stick our baked potatoes on the ends of twigs and warm them in the embers. Dom was the last to do this, so he was standing there by himself when his eyes were suddenly drawn to a darkened portion of garden on the other side of the flames. There was a woodshed over there, jammed in the corner where the garage wall connected with the holly hedge. Perhaps it was an optical effect, an image formed in the wavering heat and flickering shadows, but apparently his gaze suddenly focussed on a dark figure partly concealed in the gap between the shed and the hedge.

The chilling events of previous days no doubt played their part. But this figure was human-shaped – Dom swore that; it was also completely black, as if composed of some unearthly material. What was more, though Dom couldn't see its eyes, he knew it was staring fiercely back at him. He was so mesmerised by this that, as well as forgetting he had a spud in the fire, he also forgot that he was holding an open box of fireworks. He didn't even notice when a fleck of burning ash landed inside it. In fact, he was so frightened by the spectral form that he turned and stumbled back towards the rest of us without realising that at least five fireworks in his box were now hissing and spurting.

The entire lot would have gone up in his face had Gideon not reacted quickly, jumping forward, shouting "Gimpish features!" – his favourite phrase to describe Dom – and kicking the box out of Dom's hand. Unfortunately, though this saved Dom, it peppered the crowd with lighted fireworks. Panic and screaming ensued as, one by one, they became fountains of dazzling flame.

I saw Charlie dancing as a Mini Meteor darted around his feet. One of Clark's college friends shouted "whoooaaa!" as he ripped off his poncho and hurled it, a Telstar having landed in its hood. The bullet with *my* name on it was wide of the mark. It was a Little Demon, and it spun through the air fizzling like a stick of dynamite, before landing in the bowl of treacle, where it exploded magnificently. I'd dashed over there to escape, and though the firework didn't hit me, three great globs of red-hot treacle spattered me simultaneously – one on my coat, one on my cheek, and one in the front of my hair.

My first thought after this happened was that Dom wasn't just going to catch it from Gideon, this time he was going to catch it from me as well. But before I could say anything, everyone else started shouting at him. He blathered out his explanation, but it didn't make much sense to anyone except me. I threaded through the angry crowd to the bonfire, which had now sunk to a pile of glowing embers. Beyond it, I could clearly distinguish the gap between the hedge and the shed, and I too thought I saw a shape. But as I stared harder, I realised that what I was actually seeing was a mass of cut-down shrubbery, which had been shoved there some time ago and forgotten. Dom's eerie 'figure' was an unfortunate tangle of branches, which, when seen from a certain angle and in a certain kind of light, assumed sinister proportions.

I turned around to tell him, only to see Clark coming across the grass towards me.

"Okay young 'un?" he asked, possibly thinking the black mark on my face was a burn.

I nodded, and fingered the treacle on my cheek, which was cooling fast and already adhering to the skin.

"You'd better get up to the bathroom and wash that off quick, or you'll be taking the top layer off with it. There's some in your hair as well."

I'd have said something to Dom as I made my way back to the house, but people were still giving him the rounds of the kitchen. Charlie was standing close by, munching on a potato. He grinned at me as I passed, and for once I grinned back. It had, after all, been an amusing incident. And nobody had got hurt. Yet.

The upstairs of the Blyford house was a single passage. It led from the top of the staircase to the far end of the building, where Doctor Blyford's bedroom was located. The bathroom was half-way along it on the left. I trooped down there, scratching at the treacle and, finding it difficult enough to dislodge from my cheek, wondering how on earth I was going to remove it from my hair. Outside there was a renewed *whizzing* and *cracking*; the party was picking up its feet again.

When I reached the bathroom door, it was ajar. I hesitated to push it all the way open because there was a light on inside. I was about to knock, when I heard a rustling noise behind me. I glanced around and, entirely by accident, purely because of the position I was standing in, I was able to see straight through the partly open door of Beth's bedroom – to where she was standing nude in front of a full-length mirror.

I only saw her from behind and the side. Her dark hair hung almost to her waist, obscuring much – but not everything. Not her lovely legs, nor her firm, rounded bottom, nor the brown-tipped hemisphere of her right breast. Her skin was satin-smooth, with a peaches-and-cream glow. As I watched, stunned, she gathered up her hair and lifted it, turning her face from side to side, trying different styles. She placed one dainty foot in front of the other; an elegant pose – she was flawless, more like a sculpture than a human being.

I'd glanced at girlie mags before, but this was the first time I'd ever seen a fully developed woman naked in the flesh – and what an effect it had. Previously there'd been nothing erotic in my affections for Beth. I'd loved her passionately but confusedly – from a safe, non-lustful distance. As

104

a child, sex had always been something we sniggered at behind our hands. It got in the way of our feelings for girls rather than enhanced them. But now, in a moment like a thunderclap, everything was different. Suddenly it wasn't just my emotions that were on fire. It wasn't just my stomach that was tightening.

"You dirty little shit!" a voice said, and I was dealt a slap to the side of my head so hard that lights flashed in front of my eyes. "You fucking dirty little bastard!"

I caught a fleeting glimpse of Beth twirling around, shocked, one hand across her breasts, the other between her legs. Then a second blow caught me, this one in the mouth. It was a clenched fist and it split my lip open. I tottered sideways.

It was Mick Stone. He'd been the one in the bathroom, and he'd emerged just in time to catch me in the act.

"You dirty little shit!"

He kicked me in the left thigh, which, with his biker boots on, felt like he'd whacked me with an iron club. Grabbing me by the hair, he threw me across the landing, banging my head into the wall. It hurt like hell, but the tears stinging my eyes were tears of humiliation rather than pain. There'd be no explaining my way out of this. I'd ruined everything. The urge to flee was overwhelming. But Stone had hold of me and wouldn't release me. He clapped a hand to my throat, forcing me back against the wall, banging my head again.

"I didn't mean to …" I pleaded.

It seemed certain he was going to hit me again, but I was already bleeding copiously and maybe he felt there was no need. Instead, he jammed his fist up hard beneath my jaw, forcing my mouth closed.

"I'll bet you didn't, you lying little toad!"

"Mick, for God's sake!" Beth said. She dashed from her bedroom, hurriedly tying her dressing gown at the waist, then tugged his hands away and released me. "What the hell do you think you're doing?"

"He was watching you!"

"It was an accident," I stammered.

"Accident, my arse!" He made another grab at me. "You little shit!"

"Mick!" She pushed him backward.

"Look at him, the soft little bastard!" I was openly crying by now, which only served to increase his determination to punish me. He leaned forward, his ugly face twisted into something demonic. "Not nice when the rest of the world knows what a dirty little shit you are, is it!"

"For God's sake," she hissed. "He's only a kid."

"Not that much of a kid, clearly."

"Here, Stephen." Beth handed me a folded tissue to dab at my lip.

"Well?" he barked. "What've you got to say for yourself? Spying on my bird while she's in the altogether. Seeing everything she's got. You'd better make it good."

106

I burbled something about coming up here to go to the bathroom, but a denial of what I'd been caught doing seemed pointless. I was burning with shame and crying hard. Despite my tissue, there was snot all over my chin as well as blood. I must have looked a pathetic sight,

"You'd better go home, Stephen," Beth said. Her voice was calm but cold. "Go out the front way, so nobody sees you."

I did as she asked, sobbing all the way.

13

I explained my mangled lip to my Mum and Dad by saying that I'd slipped on the steps at the side of Dom's house. They had no reason to disbelieve me – how could I have got into a fight at my best friend's home? Dom would ask me the same thing the next day, and I'd fob him off with the same excuse, adding that that was why I'd left the party early.

This was the first day of our half-term break. We now had a week off. Normally this would be a time for celebration, but I wasn't in the mood much when Dom called for me just after ten that morning. Apparently, I'd agreed to help him clear up the firework debris from the previous night. This was the last thing I wanted, because it would take me back to their house and I didn't think I could face Beth so soon. But it was a good sign that Dom didn't know anything about what had happened; it meant the word hadn't spread.

I suggested we go down the Valley instead of tidying the garden, but Dom wasn't keen. He assured me that during the party, he'd seen a suspicious figure lurking behind the shed. I hadn't yet had the opportunity to prove to him that he'd been mistaken, but neither of us had got over the incident at Ettinshall yet and, if I was honest, I didn't particularly want to go down the Valley either. It was another wet, grey day of the sort November specialises in, so it would be particularly dank and miserable down there. In the end, we headed back towards Dom's house, he maintaining all the way that the thing he'd seen had been real, me desperately trying to think of a way to avoid spending the next few days hanging out in some place where I might meet Beth. As we reached the corner of Jubilee Crescent, Dom suggested we do some work on our bows and arrows, maybe even get them blessed in church – then we'd have a weapon with which to protect ourselves against Red Clogs. I consented eagerly, mainly because our archery practise took place on the flat grass at the top of the Valley, away from the Blyford House.

A common mistake for youngsters making bows – if they even do such zany, boy scout-type things these days – is to start out with a piece of wood that's already bow-shaped, because this gives it no tension whatsoever. Way back the previous summer, I'd been watching a television documentary about the battle of Agincourt in 1415, when eight thousand English archers massacred thirty thousand French knights, losing only a couple of hundred of their own. The programme had shown in detail how the legendary longbow was constructed. With this in mind, when Dom and I had first gone out to make our weapons, we'd cut six-foot lengths of yew, which were sturdy and straight, and had bent them backward before stringing them with fishing twine. The finished products had been so good that initially we'd had trouble drawing them. Naturally we'd had to improvise for the arrows, falling back on willow or bamboo rods, whose points we'd sharpened with a penknife. We didn't have the know-how to produce steel arrowheads, or to fletch them with real feathers. The upshot was that our bows weren't particularly accurate, but they could drive a projectile with sufficient force to smash the jack-o-lantern turnips that we'd ended up sacrificing before Halloween arrived.

Jack-o-lanterns made targets for us again, this time the old tin ones left over from the party. These were now scorched relics, but we grabbed them from the garage, took them to the top of the Valley, set them up on bricks, and launched arrows at them with fiendish glee. Whenever the arrows struck, they punctured the tins clean through, sometimes to a degree where they were difficult to extricate. We practised for most of that morning. It was strenuous exercise and made us feel strong and athletic. I imagined that I was hitting targets harder and more accurately than ever before. I fancied I could hit one from sixty, maybe seventy yards. I even suggested I could take down a moving target. Dom was awed by the mere thought. I said we needed better arrows; we should chop up the jack-o-lanterns and use the shards of metal for our arrowheads. Duck-down feathers would aid with flight and accuracy. Next time we went to Ettinshall, I declared, we'd be the hunters not the hunted.

"Hi fellas," Beth said from behind, and my macho world came tumbling down.

The arrow I'd just strung went flying in completely the wrong direction.

"Good shot," she said, approaching across the grass in an anorak and hip-hugging jeans. Sheba trotted loyally alongside her.

"Hi," Dom replied, surprised to see her, but, as always, pleased.

"Do you fancy taking Sheba down the Valley?" she said to him. "Not all the way down to the wood, just run her up and down the slope for a bit." She stuck a shapely foot out, showing a new white plimsole. "I've just bought these, and I don't want to get them mucky."

"Er sure, yeah." He took the lead and turned to me. "Coming?"

I laid my bow aside. "Why not?"

"No, you stay here, Stephen," Beth said. "Keep me company."

Dom looked puzzled, but then it seemed to occur to him that we were probably going to be discussing him – how he was getting on at his new school, that sort of thing. Even more pleased, he sauntered away down the slope, the dog gambolling ahead.

"So … can we talk?" Beth asked, once he was out of earshot.

I shrugged. "If you want to."

"Don't you think we should?"

I shuffled my feet awkwardly. "I feel … really bad about what happened."

Again, it was a mark of how society has changed. Nowadays, the main talking point of the previous night would have been the violent retribution taken against me, a thirteen-year-old. But back in those days, youngsters were routinely slapped and hit – not just by their parents and teachers, but by other kids. It was the 'moral' lapse that was the main offence; my peeking in on her while she was naked.

"It was a little bit naughty what you did," she said. "But lads will always be lads. It's not the end of the world. How are you anyway?"

I touched my lip. "Sore."

"Hmm. Well I've told Mick off. He should never have hit you like that."

"I think … well, I think he was protecting your honour."

I'd heard that phrase, 'protecting your honour', on an American Civil War movie the previous Saturday – two Confederate officers had fought a duel over a lady one of them had attempted to seduce. I was pretty sure it was an appropriate term for this situation.

Beth seemed to think so too, though she also looked a little amused.

"Surely my honour was in no danger, Stephen? On the subject of which, I take it you're not planning to brag to your friends that you saw me with no clothes on?"

I was amazed she could even ask such a thing. I shook my head adamantly. It wasn't just the embarrassment that would stem from having to admit that I'd been caught peeking, which was bad enough, and then had taken a beating for my trouble, which was even more embarrassing, but my feelings were still massively confused. I was excited by what I'd seen, but at the same time guilt-stricken. The urge to expiate myself might be satisfied by blabbing – maybe I could relieve my pain by discussing it with someone (Father Carrickfergus perhaps)? But at the same time, I felt that this was something private between Beth and I – something we shared that nobody else did – and that to make it public knowledge would cheapen it beyond reclamation.

"The main thing is we're still friends, yeah?" she said, which shocked me but in a nice sort of way.

"If you still want us to be."

"Well, it's a silly little thing and it shouldn't be allowed to spoil a good relationship, don't you agree?"

I nodded – eagerly, probably too eagerly.

She smiled. "I'll not be mentioning this again if you don't."

I assured her I wouldn't, and then, right on cue, we heard the approaching rumble of a motorbike.

"Looks like my ride's here," she said, as Stone came cruising around the corner on his bike, which was a gleaming black Norton 850. He pulled up about forty yards away on the edge of the grass, and sat waiting, his engine turning over noisily.

"You sure you're all right?" she asked.

I nodded again.

"No loose teeth or anything?"

"He doesn't hit as hard as he thinks." I glowered at Stone, who'd lifted his visor and was glowering back.

"That's the spirit," she said, before heading over there. "Just ask Dom to take Sheba home, will you?"

"Mick doesn't deserve you, Beth," I called after her.

She glanced back, looking briefly surprised. But then she smiled again. "I know."

I watched jealously as she put on the spare helmet Stone gave her and climbed onto the seat behind him. He pulled the machine round in a tight circle, fired one more baleful glare at me, and roared away.

"Just don't hurt my girl," I said, loving Beth more than I'd ever loved any human being on Earth, and, as a flipside to that coin, loathing Mick Stone with equal depth and passion. It wasn't just because of what he'd done to me the previous night; it wasn't because of that at all. Ridiculously, I now realise, though at the time it didn't seem so, and quite out of the blue, I'd come to view him as a rival who needed dispensing with.

14

It was the morning of November 14th, and Pete Tugton had only been in the ground two days when the body of Alan Richardson was found.

An old lady was walking her dog down a backstreet not far from St. Nathaniel's High School, when she saw what she first thought were the naked feet of a showroom mannequin protruding from the top of a dustbin.

The victim, who was fourteen years old, had been bludgeoned and strangled with his school tie some time the previous evening. After an attack lasting maybe ten minutes, his broken body had been stuffed unceremoniously into the bin. Given that he was not a St. Nathaniel's pupil and was found several miles from his home neighbourhood, the police search, which had been launched less than an hour after his disappearance was reported, and had continued all night, had failed to locate him. The first we learned about it was when we arrived at school the following morning and were told by our form teachers that a special assembly was being held so that the police could talk to us. Similar special assemblies were apparently being held in schools across the borough.

We filed into the main hall pale-faced. There was no more horseplay, no more impersonation of Mafia funerals. The twenty minutes that had elapsed between us first hearing about this latest tragedy and the official address, which was made from the headmaster's podium by a senior detective, was sufficient for all kinds of bone-chilling rumours to do the rounds. One held that people living near the backstreet in question had reported being disturbed around midnight by the sound of hysterical laughter. Another claimed that bloody footprints had led away from the murder scene, but that police dogs were too frightened to follow them.

The policeman who addressed us introduced himself as Detective Inspector Sterling. He was a big, broad-shouldered chap – his suit looked as though it was about to burst apart on his immense frame – with fiery-blond hair and a blond handlebar moustache. A younger detective was standing to one side, in company with Mr. Crab, our headmaster, and Father Carrickfergus.

To start with, Detective Inspector Sterling said, it must be obvious to all of us that an extremely dangerous man was on the loose in Ashburn. He didn't wish to frighten us unduly but added that it was imperative we responded to this crisis in a sensible way. The boys in particular, but also the girls, had to be extremely careful when they were out of doors – at any time of day. He didn't want us to go anywhere alone, particularly when we were walking home from school or running errands in the evening. In fact, we'd all be taking a letter home at the end of the day, which was from the police, requesting a curfew on all those under the age of sixteen. He said he knew this wasn't ideal, and that it wasn't something he had the right to impose on us, but he thought it was for the best.

There were a number of things we had to be specifically wary of. He didn't wish to "teach us to suck eggs", but it was important to once again go over the lessons we'd learned in early childhood. In no circumstances must we be drawn into conversations with adults we didn't know – and this didn't just include the usual suspects like suspicious-looking men in dirty raincoats offering us sweets or inviting us to see some puppies, it also meant clean-cut types who might stop their car to ask us directions, tradesmen arriving at our front door and asking to be let in, people claiming to be officials (doctors, police officers, social workers) but unable to prove this with ID. We were also told that we should report anyone at all who seemed to be watching us, following us, hanging around our street, or generally popping up here and there in our lives for no apparent reason – and not just those we didn't know, but also those we didn't know very well. It was vital to remember that it wasn't just strangers we had to be wary of. The murdered boys weren't babies, they were robust teenagers; they couldn't have been snatched off the streets or dragged into a car easily. There had to be some subtle way the killer had lured them.

We listened to this part of the speech with incredulity. Was he suggesting the killer might be someone close to us? He added that we mustn't assume this meant it was someone we saw all the time, like a relative or teacher, but we could probably all name men who we knew well enough to stop and chat to but who we hadn't known our whole lives. The most important thing to remember, he said, was that the sort of men who committed these crimes were not the sort we would expect. We shouldn't be watching out for some wild-eyed human wreck frothing at the mouth. He might be wearing a shirt and tie, have neatly combed hair, he might be handsome and smiling politely. In real life, monsters do not look like monsters.

"This one does," someone said from the audience.

We were seated in rows, obediently cross-legged and attentive, but now everyone glanced around. It was Colin Lapwing who'd spoken. He was at the end of my row, red-eyed and sniffling into a tissue. I didn't know at the time, but the latest victim was a cousin of his. He glanced along the line tearfully, and, when he finally located me, pointed an accusing finger.

"Ask *him*, Stephen Carter. He knows all about the monster. He's seen it. It chased him."

There was an awed hush in the hall. Detective Inspector Sterling gazed at me with interest. Mr. Crab stepped forward. For once his face wasn't like thunder; he looked astonished. Father Carrickfergus looked horrified.

Twenty minutes later, my Mum had been summoned and was sitting alongside me in the passage outside the head's office. When the door opened, Colin came out, still sniffling. His own mother was with him; she had an arm around his shoulders and was also holding a tissue to her nose.

"Would you good people like to come in now?" Mr. Crab called.

He was a large, solidly built man, and very imposing, with a head of ginger curls and thick ginger sideburns. He was known as an authority figure, and given to using the cane regularly, but on this occasion – proving that he was only a tyrant when it was necessary – he was in courteous mode. He ushered us in and pulled up seats for my Mum and I. Mrs. Juno, the deputy headmistress was also present. She smiled and nodded and fiddled nervously with the glasses that always hung from a chain around her neck. Father Carrickfergus was there too, along with the two police officers, Detective Inspector Sterling and the other one, who had a young face and short, black hair. He was introduced as Detective Constable McGrath.

Up close, everything about Detective Inspector Sterling was huge – his head, his chest, his neck, his hands. He radiated power, but it was a warm kind of power; he was like a lion, but a friendly one. He and his assistant were also seated, but no-one was behind the headmaster's desk. We were all in a kind of circle, which surprised me – I'd only ever been in this room before when there was an atmosphere of intimidation. However, I was still frightened and worried, assuming that my silence beforehand would now get me into big trouble.

There were several reasons why I hadn't told any adult what had happened to Dom and me up at Ettinshall (Dom hadn't been hauled in because Colin never mentioned his involvement, and so far, I too was keeping it quiet).

First of all, at some deep, intellectual level, I still wasn't one hundred percent convinced that I believed in Red Clogs. Oh yes, it was incredibly real to me, but I was thirteen, not eight; old enough to realise that such things shouldn't exist even if they apparently did. It was like a dark reflection of the problem we faced each Christmas – you still thought of Father Christmas as a real person, but only because you wanted to, and you certainly wouldn't admit it publicly. Secondly, there was the fear of retribution. I had a childish dread that if I grassed on Red Clogs, I'd become the sole object of his attention; from that point on, it was *me* he'd be after, nobody else. Thirdly, if I'd admitted that I'd been up to Ettinshall alone, or even with Dom, it would be owning up to my parents that I'd been lying to them and hadn't been spending all my time at Dom's house. Even the gentle way I'd been received into the headmaster's office hadn't made me realise that we were long past the stage where petty deceptions by children were an issue.

Anyway, I told them everything – all about the trip to the colliery. Half-way through, I even disclosed that Dom had been up there too. It had quickly become difficult to pretend I'd been alone – they clearly didn't believe it. After I'd finished, the two policemen conferred for a couple of minutes, then Detective Inspector Sterling turned and addressed me in a grown-up, pally sort of way.

"Stephen … that's what I call you, yeah? Stephen or Steve?"

"Er … Steve."

"Steve … it has occurred to you that you were probably quite scared at the time because of what's been happening? What you saw and heard might just have been figments of your imagination."

"But Dom saw and heard it too."

"There's a thing called 'mass hysteria'. You ever been told about that?"

I shook my head.

He explained: "You get a group of people together who are all frightened or upset by the same thing, particularly if it's something that isn't there, and the next thing you know – they actually start to see and hear it. All at the same time. It's strange, but it really happens. It's been recorded on a number of occasions. It's like a mass hallucination."

"They all see and hear *exactly* the same thing?" I said sceptically.

"Not necessarily, but do you and Dom know that you saw and heard *exactly* the same thing? Have you compared notes?"

"I suppose not," I said. This was true, and it was quite a revelation when I considered it.

He smiled. "Think of this as a kind of nightmare, which, Heaven knows, is hardly surprising after what's been going on. I understand that one of the boys killed was a close friend of yours?"

I nodded again.

"Well, I can assure you that we're doing everything we can to catch whoever did it. You know how many officers are now assigned to this case? – fifty. I've never known so many. And all of them top lads. I promise you, Steve, we're going to get whoever's responsible for this."

"But Red Clogs …"

"Red Clogs is a story, a fable. It's understandable that you and your friends have been frightened by it. This is a new experience for you all. God knows, it'd be a new experience for any kid. But it's probably not a good idea to keep talking about this monster as if he's real. Remember what I said in your assembly? The real murderer's most likely to be someone who seems completely normal to you."

And that was it. No clip behind the ear, no telling-off of any sort. He even promised me that he wouldn't go and speak to Doctor Blyford about Dom's involvement, because he said there was probably no need for it. He winked, and the interview was over.

I sat outside in the passage while my Mum went to use the lavatory. The headmaster's door had been left open a crack, and I overheard the adults summing things up.

"The truth is, and I wouldn't admit it to the lad," Sterling said. "But it's probably a good thing if they believe it's some kind of supernatural entity."

"How can that be?" Mr. Crab asked.

"Well … you know how it is with youngsters. To them, mass murderers aren't real. Grown-ups don't do things like this to children, hence they're not frightened of grown-ups. If they think it's some kind of monster though, they're more likely to heed what we say and stay indoors.

"Surely that's deceiving them?"

"I'm not saying we spread these stories ourselves, but perhaps we shouldn't discourage them. At the end of the day, even to me, there's an eerie kind of resonance in what that lad said. Many of the injuries on the victims are consistent with being kicked or stamped. They were beaten as well of course – bricks, pipes, whatever blunt instrument came to hand. One was strangled too, one stabbed – in fact 'disembowelled' would be closer to the mark."

"Good Lord."

"But there have been no sexual assaults that we're aware of."

"Isn't that a good thing?" Mr. Crab said.

"It makes our job harder because it removes motive. There's been no sexual interference with any of the bodies, either before or after death. It's very strange."

"How near are you to catching him?"

"We're making some ground. As I said to the lad, there's a lot more manpower available to us now that it's clear this maniac's going to continue. I hate to admit it, but there's almost certainly going to be another one unless we get him quickly. Initially we were working on the basis it might be a vagrant, someone passing through. But we've rounded up just about every homeless body in the borough, which in truth is only a few. We've also questioned anyone we know with form for molesting or assaulting children. None of them are in the frame, but at least we're crossing names off the list. Whoever he is, he's elusive. What was it that lad said … 'only his feet are real, the rest of him is made of mist'?" Detective Inspector Sterling chuckled grimly. "That would fit the bill too. He keeps slipping through our fingers like an honest-to-goodness ghost."

When my Mum and I went home, those words were still ringing in my head.

Like an honest-to-goodness ghost.

For all the reassurances the policeman had given me, there was now no doubt in mind what it was that faced us here.

15

Despite the airy confidence with which Detective Inspector Sterling had dismissed my story, I stood in our back garden the following Saturday and gazed up to the distant wilderness that was Ettinshall, where a straggling line of tiny figures, police officers and their dogs, were combing the slag.

If they ever found anything, I wasn't told about it. There were lots of references to the murders in the press, but I didn't read newspapers at that age; I saw the occasional headline and spotted grainy photographs of Dean Stanton, Pete Tugton or Alan Richardson, but I had no enthusiasm to look further. Stories reached me through my Mum that Pete's family were suffering badly since his death; his father had been out in the street a few times, drunk and shouting about it, and his mother had – in my Mum's words – "gone funny"; she would apparently stop people in town and talk to them as if Pete was still alive, often with a beatific smile on her face. Such things were horrible and tragic, and made me realise even more than the memory of seeing Pete's body what a disaster we were in the midst of.

In spite of the wide interest in the case, the newspapers had nothing substantial to report for the next month, aside from rumour and counter-rumour, and these were never less than lurid. The story about the hysterical laughter at the scene of

Alan Richardson's murder made it onto the front pages, along with new, equally disturbing tales: Satanic symbols had been left next to the bodies; a tall, pale-faced young man had been knocking on the doors of a local council estate, asking for cups of water – most people sent him away, but one old lady lured him into her lounge and went to call the police, only to return and find the young man gone, the words "your grandson is next" written on the mirror in human excrement; a clairvoyant had tried to locate the murderer through a spiritualist session, and received a parcel through the post the very next day, containing a large, black spider.

None of these were true, as it transpired, but they helped to reinforce the climate of fear – which in some ways was good. I'm sure there were no further developments that month because almost no youngsters at all were allowed outside after school. When darkness fell, the streets and avenues of our town were deserted. I was only allowed up to Dom's if my Dad could drive me, and vice versa for Dom. He came down to mine once, but our significantly smaller house didn't offer much scope for 'playing indoors', so usually we finished up at his. We'd spend most of our evenings in the dining room there, though in truth it hadn't been used as a real dining room for many years. It was a large, wood-panelled chamber, which could have been very handsome, yet, like so many other parts of the Blyford house, it was in a state of semi-deterioration. It was drab and dusty, and though it still had a central dining table, this was piled high with boxes of junk, as were all four of the room's corners.

With nothing better to do, we'd close ourselves in there and try to distract our thoughts from the pitch-darkness beyond the curtained window by skewering conkers and threading them (despite the conker season now being long past), by playing trump cards or even talking about Christmas and what we hoped to get – though Christmas seemed a long way off at that moment. Back in 1974, the television schedules weren't filled with Christmas adverts once November 5th had passed, and the shops didn't dress themselves up with tinsel as soon as they'd sold out of fireworks, so it seemed there were many long, gloomy schooldays and even longer, gloomier nights before that sparkling time of year would arrive.

We occasionally discussed Red Clogs, but there was no longer any nonsensical talk about going hunting him with our bows, or getting our arrows blessed in church. Now that we *knew* he was real rather than simply feared it, he was a far more ominous spectre at our shoulder. As ever, Gideon found these conversations tiresome. At fifteen, his nocturnal activities had also been curtailed by the crisis, so he'd often join us in the dining room, and would wildly insist that Red Clogs was kid's stuff, telling us to grow up, to stop scaring ourselves to death over nothing. When we mentioned the terrifying apparition we'd seen at the colliery, he scoffed, assuring us we'd been mistaken.

Occasionally on these nights, our fears and frustrations – not to mention the cabin fever that naturally arose with being cooped up in that single room all the time – would boil over into frenziedly silly games: Blind Man's Buff in the dark, which was even more fun if all parties played it armed with rolled up magazines; Scalextric, which we hadn't played for years, but where the object was no longer to win the race but to stage epic crashes and take out as many track-side figures as possible; the construction of World War Two dioramas, in which we'd use a cigarette lighter and lashings of red paint to turn huge swathes of our Airfix soldiers into ultra-realistic corpses. We were all still in a mild state of shock to be caught in the middle of this true-life horror story, but gradually – as happens with youngsters – time passed and because there were no further incidents, our thoughts began to return to normal.

Beth, who'd been away on a course, returned in late November, which cheered me no end, even though I only usually saw her in passing. Occasionally, she'd stick her head into the dining room and ask if we wanted a cup of coffee, or, after Clark briefly broke off from his studies to fix a portable TV in there for us (which never worked particularly well, thanks to it having a coat-hanger for an aerial), she'd pop in to watch some TV show that her dad didn't want to watch in the lounge – *Monty Python* on Mondays, *The Two Ronnies* on Tuesdays, *Benny Hill* on Wednesdays, *Top of the Pops* on Thursdays. Dom enjoyed her company on these occasions almost as much as I did. He always seemed inordinately glad to see her. I suppose she'd become a mother figure to him; there were some times when I thought he was going to sit on her knee.

Of course, now and then Mick Stone would be with her. He and I had never repaired our damaged relationship, mainly because neither of us wanted to. I kept out of his way and he restricted his assaults on me to the purely verbal. But this, in its way, was no less unpleasant. He'd taken to calling me 'Gobby' – repeatedly, at every opportunity, in an apparent effort to cement it into everyone's consciousness. Clearly, this was to be my new nickname. Once spring came and the horror was over, and lots of kids would start socialising outdoors again, this was how I'd be referred to – in the place where I'd lived and been happy all my life. And all thanks to a bloke who up until a month ago had been a complete outsider.

'Gobby'. Because he said I had a big mouth.

The irony was that he had an immensely big mouth himself, and thick, rubbery, 'Mick Jagger' lips, which increased the illusion. When he laughed or shouted, it was like looking down the Mersey Tunnel. He might have been older, bigger and much beefier than me, but you can only take so much abuse. You can only sit back for so long and be mocked and menaced in a place where previously you've felt perfectly safe – especially when the person doing it is someone who also happens to be standing between you and the love of your life. I was only young, you understand, and very naïve, but I knew a time was fast approaching when I'd have to shut that Mersey Tunnel mouth for good.

In the meantime, November had come to an end.

Almost immediately, the atmosphere in Ashburn seemed to change. The Advent calendars went up (which was an exciting event in itself, despite there not being any chocolate bribes behind the little doors in those days), and festive lights appeared all over the town's shopping streets. At last it felt as if that long, dismal autumn was over, especially a couple of days later when the temperature plummeted and there was a severe frost. Very appropriately, it was December 6th, the feast of St Nicholas, when we had our first heavy snowfall. It had been bitterly cold all day at school, the sky slate-grey, the frost staying white on the roofs of the buildings and the grass of the playing fields. When you went outside, even if bundled up in a Parka and gloves, your breath smoked heavily. By home time it was already pitch-dark, and heavy, feather-sized flakes were falling in a steady cascade. With the last murder nearly a month ago, and a gradual easing of tension, a number of parents had stopped picking their kids up from school. Mine hadn't. I still had to wait at the school gate, along with Dom, who we usually gave a ride to. En route home, it was more than frustrating to gaze through the car window and see gangs of kids racing up and down the pavements, snowballing. My Mum watched us through the rear-view mirror. She'd already realised that it was going to be difficult keeping us indoors now that Christmassy weather had arrived. But of course, mums being what they are, she was determined to try.

"It's early winter yet," she said dismissively. "This will have thawed in a couple of days. So, don't be letting yourselves get carried away."

But it didn't thaw.

It snowed the next day as well, so hard, and creating drifts so deep that it disrupted routine activities like bus and train services. We saw plenty of snowball action in the schoolyard, but the one thing Dom and I really wanted to do was go sledging in the Valley. The previous night, my Mum had ruled it out completely, and in fact had refused me permission to go up to Dom's at all because she'd said that she didn't trust us to stay indoors. In conciliation, she'd added that I could go sledging the following Saturday. It would be safer then because there'd be lots of other people doing the same thing. But that was the problem – all the other people. The slopes would be crowded and the running surfaces ruined. Dom and I knew that if we wanted to get some quality sledging in for ourselves, it would have to be that second night, which was a Friday.

I worked on my Mum from the moment I got home from school, begging her to let me go up to Dom's, promising that we wouldn't leave his house. Eventually my Dad came in from work, beating flakes from the shoulders of his overcoat. Too weary to fight after a long day at the office and a long, frustrating journey home, he said: "For God's sake, let the boy go. He'll be safe indoors.

No-one in the right mind would be out in this weather."

"That's just it," my Mum replied. "It isn't someone in the right mind, is it?"

"I'll drop him off at the door. If he doesn't take his sledge with him, he's hardly likely to go sledging, is he?"

She grumpily consented. Of course, what neither she nor my Dad knew was that, while my sledge was left locked in our garage, Dom's garage, which couldn't be locked because it was too old, contained three sledges.

It was just after seven when my Dad dropped me off. As usual, he hung around for a little while, the engine rumbling, to ensure I got up the drive safely. Dom, typically, almost blew it by answering the door in a thick sweater and bob-cap, but my Dad was either too short-sighted to spot this or in too a big hurry to be off because, once I'd gone inside, he tore away, snow spurting from his tyres.

It was considerably easier for Dom and Gideon to sneak out than it was for me. Doctor Blyford was already sofa-bound and settling into his mid-evening inertia, which meant he'd be unlikely to notice our absence even if we left the house shouting with excitement – which Dom almost did, an injudicious act that earned him a kick in the pants from Gideon; and, with it being Friday evening, neither Clark nor Beth were home, both having headed to the nightclubs in town.

We legged it down Jubilee Crescent, each one of us hauling a sledge. Needless to say, Gideon had the state-of-the-art one: a streamlined PVC affair, which resembled a curved surfboard. Mine was an older model, a sturdy wooden one with steel runners, while Dom's was battered and homemade; it looked suspiciously like an improvised tea-tray to me, but apparently he was emotionally attached to it and didn't want to use any of the others (an attitude I suspect he'd cultivated having never been allowed to use any of the others because Gideon and Clark always monopolised them).

We got to the top of the Valley, and a majestic scene lay before us. It had stopped snowing about an hour earlier, and now the cloud-cover had broken, allowing moonlight to shimmer down through air as sharp as crystal, and glint back from an unbroken blanket of white. Far below, the skeletal trees of Scubby Hollow were like charcoal etchings on pristine paper. At the very bottom of the Valley, we could even see the silver-grey ribbon of the river, which was frozen solid. Hooting with joy, we set about finding the fastest slope. There were plenty to choose from. The snow was soft and dry as powder, so even the shallower slopes – the "nursery slopes" as we scathingly referred to them, thinking of the hordes of once-a-year wonders who'd be here tomorrow afternoon – allowed exhilaratingly swift passage.

There's almost no greater feeling than hurtling down a snowy hill, the bracing winter air hitting your face so fiercely that it makes your eyes water, leaping over hidden tussocks of grass, the dark line of the woods racing up to greet you (and you

133

never quite sure if you're going to stop in time before you strike it) – a sensation enhanced if you go down on your chest, which was the way we always did it. When little kids and old grannies sledge, they sit upright and hold the reins for dear life, almost like they're riding a horse. But we preferred the more masculine "freestyle" method: lying flat, controlling the sledge by gripping the upward curves of its runners, one in each fist.

We'd been down four or five times before we collided in a massive pile-up near the bottom and, once we'd untangled ourselves, lay in the snow in a laughing, pink-faced heap.

"Shit!" Dom suddenly said, sitting bolt-upright. "What about Red Clogs?"

Talk about putting a downer on things.

I sat upright too, gazing at the nearby woods. From this close, you could see the white pathways snaking through the naked, frozen tangles. But if some menacing figure was flitting about in there, coming closer and closer by sneaking from tree to tree, we wouldn't necessarily spot it.

"That's complete bollocks!" Gideon snapped impatiently. "Look, I happen to know there's no such thing as Red Clogs."

"Three lads have died," I reminded him, suddenly not liking the way our voices echoed in the night air.

"Yeah, at the hands of an escaped loony. Look, whoever it was is long gone. There's no-one here but us."

So, we got on with it, just the three of us – climbing the slope, sledging down it, climbing again, sledging down again, our excited squeals ringing over that icy, silent terrain. The thought of Red Clogs preyed on me a little; even this much fun couldn't eliminate the dreadful memories of a month ago. But we were thoroughly enjoying ourselves, and nothing bad seemed to be happening, and soon our guard dropped. You need to throw yourself back to childhood to understand this. Everything now looked very different from the way it had in October and November; it felt different, it even smelled different. To our scatter-brained perception – the rotten leaves and dank shadows had gone, and were replaced by frosty twigs and a bright, moonlit snowscape we almost didn't recognise. It was another place now, and a much safer one.

So, when I say we got on with it, I mean we *really* got on with it.

Concentrating on the same downhill trails over and over again, our runners flattened and smoothed the snow, compressing it until it was so slippery that we could have ridden down on plastic bags. With each descent we travelled further and further across the bottom of the Valley, getting closer and closer to the trees, until at last we were penetrating into Scubby Hollow itself, winding our reckless way along its paths, still hooting with laughter.

I was deep into the little wood when I almost ran someone down.

In the midst of all that giddiness, it was a horrific shock.

I blasted downhill, the wind buffeting my face, the treeline coming on at pace. I picked my entry-point and then was swerving along the snowy track with that immense skill that only youngsters who've done this many times before can possess. And suddenly he was there in front of me, a black shape – legs spread, arms spread, blocking my progress. With a wild shout, I yanked the sledge left – and sailed through the undergrowth, smashing one wall of frost-thick bracken after another, ice crystals filling my eyes and mouth. At last I hit a root and turned over, and then I was rolling. Through sheer adrenaline I felt no pain. Instead, I jumped to my feet – but initially I was disoriented by the mesh of snow-covered branches that caged me.

A hand fell on my shoulder.

I gave a shriek that must have been heard up on Jubilee Crescent.

"You plank! It's only me!"

I glanced up and saw a familiar grinning ape-face.

Charlie's arrival cheered me up, mainly because I felt safer now that there were four of us instead of three. Of course, we only had three sledges. The solution to this, Gideon said, was to play an "even more fun game" in which we'd sledge down into Scubby Hollow three at a time, and the fourth one would hide in the trees and launch snowball ambushes. We'd take it in turns to be the ambusher. I wasn't hugely enthusiastic about this. It meant that someone would always have to be on his own down in Scubby Hollow, and surprise-surprise, I was picked first.

I peered enviously out through the trees as the other three toiled back up the slope, dragging their sledges. It seemed to take an age, and soon a tomb-like quiet had settled around me. But then they all came shooting back down again, and I danced from path to path, slamming snowballs onto their heads and bodies from point-blank range, and in actual fact it *was* a fun game. I was the ambusher for the first few times, before someone else took over. By the time it was Gideon's turn, we were fully into it, having lost all sense of time or place. I hurried back up the slope, with Dom just ahead of me and Charlie about thirty yards behind. Dom and I reached the top at just the same time – and were stopped in our tracks by the sight of Doctor Blyford's Bentley sitting at the end of Jubilee Crescent, its engine chugging.

The driver's window had been wound down, and Doctor Blyford was watching us. He beckoned to Dom, who let the rope of his sledge drop and went dolefully forward.

I'd never seen Doctor Blyford angry before. He rarely showed any emotion; it was almost as though he was indifferent to the rest of the world. But I could tell he was angry now; his pale brow had furrowed, and his grey lips quivered.

"You've deceived me, Dominic," he said quietly.

Dom hung his head.

"Not only that, you've also defied me. And in doing so, you've put yourself and your friend in grave danger."

I heard feet plodding up the slope behind us. It was Charlie. I furtively signalled him to back away, which he quickly did, hunkering down and sliding out of sight on his bottom.

"Look Dad," Dom tried to explain, "I know you're cross, but …"

"Don't lie to me, Dominic. Whatever you're about to say, I know it will be a lie, so please don't bother. I told you to stay in the house or garden until this horrible crisis is resolved. You're *all* supposed to stay in your houses, including you, Stephen."

I hung my head too.

"Dad, we were just sledging."

"I'm not blind, Dominic. But last night you assured me that, even though the snow has come, you'd be staying inside or around the house once it got dark. You said I didn't need to worry about you. You even got uppity about it, saying you had common sense and that you weren't a child anymore. Well it seems you are still a child, Dominic. Very much so. In addition, you're a child who's made his father late. I've been called unexpectedly to a meeting at the hospital. I've spent ten minutes looking all around the house and garden to let you know I was going. When I saw your tracks leading up Jubilee Crescent, I didn't want to believe it. I never thought a son of mine could be so stupid and mule-headed. On the subject of which, where's Gideon? Is he here with you?"

"He's at Charlie's," Dom said quickly. "He's all right there, isn't he? They're indoors."

Doctor Blyford didn't look as though he entirely believed this but, short of getting out of his car and searching the Valley himself, he probably didn't feel he had much choice.

"Take your sledges back to the house, right now. Both of you."

We did as we were told, the Bentley crawling behind us.

When we arrived, Doctor Blyford wound his window down again. "Stephen, get in if you please. I'm taking you home. Dominic, go to your room."

This wasn't the first time since the murders had started that he'd given me a lift home, even though my house was only a short distance away. I usually enjoyed it: it was warm and pleasant inside the Bentley, its upholstery of leather, its dashboard and side-panels made from shiny walnut. But on this occasion, there was a chill silence. Doctor Blyford didn't look at me once but drove straight to my front door and applied the handbrake. I thanked him politely and got out, expecting him to turn the engine off and get out as well, so that he could report to my Mum and Dad. But he didn't.

He simply said: "Go home, Stephen. I have to say, I'm very disappointed in you."

As I closed the door behind me, he drove away.

16

It occurred to me later that night that the only reason Doctor Blyford might not have reported me to my parents was because he hadn't had time – I'd heard him say he was already late for a meeting. But he didn't report me the next day either. I hovered nervously around our house, waiting for the phone to ring, but a call never came. By lunchtime I was feeling a little better about this, but also a touch despondent because, though Doctor Blyford hadn't rung, Dom hadn't rung either, which suggested he was still in the doghouse. Shortly after lunch, I put my coat and gloves on, and took my sledge to the Valley. My Mum was still reluctant to let me go, even though it was midday on a Saturday. It was crisply cold outside, a pearlescent sky arching over the snow-covered countryside, and there were dozens of people out enjoying it, so she didn't have much of an argument.

There was no sign of Dom when I got there. But as I'd feared, the amateurs had arrived in droves: dads in jumpers and scarves, behaving even more excitedly than the Eskimo-clad tots they had with them; older couples in snow boots and balaclavas, watching fondly as they stood arm-in-arm at the top of the slope; gangs of older teens who I recognised from some of the rougher estates further into town, and who I just knew were going to be a problem in the future if they were only now discovering the wondrous playground that was the Valley. One clown had even arrived with a pair of skis. This was Mr. Hargreaves; he lived in the next street to us and was part of that early-70s jet-set who were always something to do with the media and tended to holiday in San Tropez in summer and Biarritz in winter, or so they'd have you believe. He had longish brown hair, tanned skin and a penchant for patterned shirts, flared pants and gold medallions; even now, the top part of his ski-jacket was unzipped so that you could see his neck chain. A few girls in the neighbourhood had a thing for him (which he loved), despite him being married (which didn't concern him in the least – you never saw him with his wife anyway), and even now were standing *ooohing* and *ahhhing* as he displayed his form on his own homemade piste, ripping it open to its grassy roots in the process.

The only person there I felt like socialising with was Gary, though, under his mother's thumb as ever, he didn't reciprocate. He had a couple of kids with him whom I didn't know – two boys slightly younger than us, both very studious looking, wearing duffle-coats and thick-lensed spectacles. I learned that they were Paul and Tim Prendergast, sons of his mother's friend, who'd left home due to her husband's "intellectual cruelty" and, virtually uninvited, had moved in with Gary's family for a few weeks. I couldn't imagine that this arrangement would suit Gary's notoriously neurotic dad very much, especially with Christmas coming; not that he'd have much say in the matter. But neither could I imagine that it would suit Gary. He was clearly doing his best to entertain the twosome, but by their unsmiling manner and cool responses to his every quip, it was an uphill struggle. Despite this, he wasn't pleased to see me. I voluntarily attached myself to their dull little band, and we sledged alongside each other a couple of times, but it was a forced atmosphere of jollity. The Prendergasts, taking their lead from Gary, soon gave up all pretence of being interested in anything I said, and stood talking quietly together, ignoring the both of us; they even stopped taking turns on the sledges. The inevitable then happened – we'd just got to the bottom of the slope again when Gary asked me to go away.

"It's nothing personal, Steve," he struggled to explain. "It's just … well, you know what Mum's like. If she turns up and sees I'm with you, she'll go crazy."

"Do you have to do every single thing she tells you?" I asked, which was fairly short-sighted of me given that I was currently in the doldrums thanks to the disobedience Dom and I had shown the previous night.

Gary shrugged. "She just thinks you guys are bad news."

"Why?"

"I don't know."

"And you'd rather hang out with these wet lettuces?"

"Well you'd rather hang out with Dominic bloody Blyford! Who, this time last year, we *both* reckoned was Weirdo of the Year!"

He was right of course. Startling, almost unexplainable changes had occurred in our little demographic over the autumn. As a group, Pete, Gary and I had been inseparable since nursery age. Last summer, we'd never have imagined that the whole thing could fall apart so quickly and spectacularly. But I still thought he was overreacting.

"No-one told you to piss off, Gary."

"You didn't need to, did you," he said. And then, rather wild eyed, he added: "That's how Pete felt too."

"Don't you dare bring Pete into this," I said, stunned.

"He felt he wasn't wanted anymore, and that's why he died."

"That's bollocks!" I shouted.

"No, it isn't!" he shouted back, looking at the floor rather than at me. "Everyone's saying it!"

Even now it amazes me how swiftly a mild disagreement became so irretrievable.

In his efforts to justify his craven behaviour, Gary had fired an incredibly cheap shot, which hurt me at a deep, emotional level. I was literally spitting with rage. I called him a coward and a weakling, adding that if he ever spoke to me again it would be too soon. I rounded my tirade off by chucking a V-sign at the Prendergast boys at the top of the slope, who only now seemed to be finding us an object of interest. But my conscience had been pricked, and my anger didn't last. Throughout November I'd been tormented by the secret fear that Pete's death had been partly my fault. With the excitement of the snow and the rapid approach of Christmas, it had started to fade, but now it flared up again.

I made my way to the top of the Valley and sat alone on a tree stump, not exactly oblivious to the excited shrieks filling the air yet feeling even more disconsolate because of them – not only did I feel crap for personal reasons, but the whole of this wonderful snowy day was being totally wasted. I must have stayed there, watching everyone else have fun, for at least another two hours; a lonely, marginalised figure. When Gary and his chums trooped past on their way home – the Prendergasts in front, talking confidentially together, Gary sloping along behind with a silly grin on his face and his hands in his pockets – none of them even looked at me.

It was late afternoon before a real friend at last showed up. It was Sheba, and she came scuttling over the snow, whining and thrusting her wet nose into my hands, before rearing up on her hind legs and lapping at my face.

"Whoa, whoa, Sheeb!" I said, laughing and standing, assuming this meant that Dom had finally arrived – only for a snowball to whack me hard on the nose.

It was a large one, and it had been thrown with such force and accuracy that it brought tears to my eyes. When I glanced up, Mick Stone was coming along the top of the slope towards me. As always, he was in his denims and leathers, and his steel-tipped motorbike boots. On this occasion he was also carrying a dog lead.

"Stupid mutt wouldn't come back when I called her," he said.

Even now Sheba shied away from him, circling around behind me as if for protection.

"Come here, you stupid bitch!" he bellowed.

She slunk across towards him, and he fastened the lead to her collar with unnecessary roughness, before slapping her hard on the haunches, causing her to yelp.

"All right Gobby?" he eventually said. "On your own today, are you? Guess that's what happens when you let your mates catch it for you."

"Where's Dom?" I asked.

"Stuck in his bedroom for the foreseeable. Come on, you stupid, hairy-arsed mutt!" Sheba had come pleadingly over to me again, and he yanked her savagely backward. "Last time I agree to take you out."

"She doesn't need the lead on," I said. "She's very obedient if you treat her properly."

"And what would you know, Gobby? You don't even treat your mates proper."

"How long's he in his bedroom for?"

"Like I said, the foreseeable. At least the rest of this weekend. Mind you, suits me and the Duchess fine." As part of the view he held of himself that he was a working-class rough diamond who was teaching a well brought-up lady the ways of the real world, Stone had taken to calling Beth "the Duchess" – only when she

145

wasn't there, of course. "Clark's gone out, Gideon and that baboon-faced mate of his have gone to a disco, and Doc Blyford's gone to a do as well. So, it means we've got the house to ourselves tonight. Know what I mean, Gobby?" He winked nastily. "While sneaky little gits like you are peeping round doors, blokes like me are getting the real action."

He hauled the dog back up the hill, and I turned away, too pained by his latest victories over me to watch him any longer.

"Hey Gobby!" he shouted.

I glanced around – and another snowball hit me in the face. Again, it had been thrown with stinging force. When I wiped the snow away, I saw that there were a couple of pebbles lodged in it. I touched my lip, which was bleeding again.

With a mocking laugh, he strode out of sight, the dog slinking at his heels.

17

Doctor Who that evening was the last episode of a story called *Planet of the Spiders*.

In it, the heroic Time Lord took a terrible risk by going head-to-head with a gigantic, super-intelligent arachnid even though he knew it would kill him. His purpose was not just to destroy another enemy of the universe, but to prove to himself that he could face something he'd lived in personal fear of, and thus move on to his next incarnation without questions about his courage and abilities.

It set me thinking – in a crazy sort of way really, but you need to understand that I'd tolerated as much as I could from Mick Stone. He'd appeared from nowhere about a month ago and had basically ruined my life – not just because of the way he treated me. That was bad enough, but that was the sort of casual bullying that went on all the time in those days, mainly because there was never an adult there to stop it, and also because it was the perceived function of older kids with regard to younger kids; every generation did it to the next one down – it was just a fact of life. But with Stone it went much deeper than that. Until he'd come swaggering along, I'd been going through my own personal enlightenment – discovering one exciting new thing after another, not just about the world around me, but about myself. Now it was all tainted. My passion for Beth was soured in the worst possible way; I could never be in her presence without him being there too; I couldn't even dream about her without seeing his brutish face looking over her shoulder. By the same token, he was obliterating my self-esteem. Like other lads of my age, I was suddenly no longer part of those gaggles of tiny children who ran around our neighbourhood like manic geese. Okay, I still built treehouses and made bows and arrows, but these weren't a childish game – these were cool things to do. They showed I wasn't frightened of heights, or of getting my hands dirty. By involving myself in these pursuits, I was asserting my credentials as a non-wimp. But Stone had tarnished this as well. By christening me Gobby, he'd belittled me in the eyes of all those I knew. The repeated throwing of snowballs in my face was an open challenge to which, of course, I couldn't respond. The mocking tone, the open dislike – they lessened me so much at a time when, more than anything else, I wanted to big myself up. It was impossible to endure this. Just as Doctor Who had done, I knew that I couldn't move onto the next stage of my life without taking drastic action.

However, once *Who* had finished and I'd had my tea, and I asked my Dad to give me a lift up to Dom's that evening, I still wasn't one hundred percent sure I could go through with the scheme I was hatching. This was because I was frightened; but I'm not sure which I was more frightened of – the scheme failing or the scheme being successful.

I now look back and assume that the incidents of the previous two months had slightly unhinged me. As a grown-up, it's impossible to recall the events of this particular night and not suspect that merely to believe what I apparently believed I was not emotionally damaged. But remember that, while to adults Red Clogs might just be another ghost story, and a rather silly one, we'd actually seen and heard him. So, we didn't just think he was real, we *knew* it.

Combine that with the religious rationalisation Father Carrickfergus had offered after Pete's memorial service – *"I promise you children that nothing in God's creation exists without having a purpose. Everything happens for a reason. Even the most malevolent things will lead ultimately to a greater good"* – and this entire fanciful business didn't just look as though it was grounded in reality, it looked predestined.

My Dad dropped me off at the bottom of Dom's main drive. I hesitated before walking up to the front door. The night-sky was clear, but conversely this meant that the temperature had plunged even more since the afternoon. A freezing mist now hung among the snow-laden trees. The only vehicle on the drive was Stone's Norton 850, which suggested that what he'd said about Doctor Blyford going out was true. Just to be on the safe side, I walked around the exterior of the largely darkened house. From above, I saw light issuing from Dom's bedroom; his penance was still ongoing. At ground level, the only light came from the lounge window, beyond which the curtains hadn't been drawn properly. I crept up to it so that my feet wouldn't crunch in the snow and peeked through the misted glass. Stone was in there alone, stripped to his t-shirt and jeans. He'd taken his boots off and was seated on the carpet in front of the fire, sipping from a can of beer as he watched the television. There was no sign of Beth, but she would be around somewhere – at least, I hoped she would, because now that I was here and could see my enemy up close, my desire for revenge faltered. He'd be no pushover for anyone, Mick Stone. He had a V-shaped upper body; his bare arms were thick with muscle. It had all been silly nonsense, I decided. I'd forget everything else and just go up to see Dom – we could have a game of trump cards in his bedroom.

I padded back round to the front door and rang the bell. It was Stone who answered.

"And what do you want, Gobby?"

"Is it okay if I come in – I mean, while Doctor Blyford's not here?"

"No can do, Gobby. Dom's incommunicado."

"Can we ask Beth?"

"Beth's in the bath." He smirked. "Can't risk letting someone like you in the house when she's knocking around in the nuddy, can we?"

"Can't you just go up and ask her? I'll wait here."

"No way, pal. Don't want to disturb her when she's beautifying herself for me, do I. Anyway, I'm in charge while she's not here, and I've made an executive decision." I was half-way down the drive when he called after me. "Hey Gobby!"

I looked back, hoping he'd changed his mind.

A snowball exploded in my face.

With a laugh, he closed the door.

Maybe a minute passed as I stood there tingling. Then I scooped some snow up, packed it into a missile, and lobbed it at the lounge window. It thudded on the glass. The curtain was immediately yanked back, and Stone appeared. He gazed out at me, more surprised than angry. From the angle he was at, he could see clear down to the drive, where I was standing.

I kicked his motorbike over.

It landed in snow, so it wasn't a heavy impact. To make up for this, I backheeled its headlight, shattering it, and then jumped on the bodywork with both feet. I glanced back again, but Stone had already vanished. A light came on in the hall. The front door banged open.

"You fucking little bastard!" he screamed.

But he didn't come immediately outside; he was climbing into his boots first, which gave me a little extra time. I picked a large stone up from the side of the drive, and dropped it onto his bike's fuel tank, which split wide open.

Stone howled as though in agony.

Then I was running – down the drive, turning sharp left into Jubilee Crescent and on towards the top of the Valley.

"You little gobby bastard!" he shrieked, charging into the road behind me.

I guess he imagined he would catch me easily, even though I had a good fifty-yard lead. But perhaps he'd forgotten, or more likely didn't know, that I was an athlete – captain of the school Rugby League team – and that I trained three lunchtimes a week. As well as speed, I had endurance, and easily made it to the top of the Valley ahead of him.

This would be the difficult moment. I'd damaged his pride and joy, but would he really want to follow me from this point? Might he be content to wait until the next time we met? To be sure, I stopped and grabbed up another couple of snowballs. Stone came in sight, and I lobbed them both. The first skimmed the top of his head as he ducked, but the second smacked him right in the middle of his face.

"You long-haired shithouse!" I shouted, quoting freely from my Dad's vocabulary whenever a pop star was being interviewed on the TV and he thought I wasn't listening.

I ran again, this time down the slope. From the vociferous swearing, there was now no question of him not following me.

Yet again, the benighted Valley was an awesome sight. As well as the snow, its lower section lay under a cowl of frigid white mist, only the claw-like tips of the trees protruding through its ceiling. It looked extraordinarily spooky, but that was the idea.

I slipped and tripped every foot of that frantic descent, but my momentum kept me going downhill. When I reached the treeline, I darted along the first path I came to, my face speckled with hot sweat, my breath coming in thick, foamy clouds. Stone was still close behind, screaming about what he was going to do to me. I took a couple of indiscriminate turns to try and disorient him, but it disoriented me as well. The mist in the heart of Scubby Hollow was so dense you could almost touch it – it was silver in colour, shimmering with the billions of ice crystals suspended in it.

Only because I'd virtually grown up down there was I able to find my way through to Hill Bank Close and the river. When I reached the bridge, I stopped – I held my breath, but the pounding of my heart sounded deafening. Stone wasn't far away. The crunching of his feet drew slowly closer. He was muttering under his breath, something like "idiot, fucking idiot!" I wondered if he was still talking about me, or whether he was criticising himself for being lured down here while wearing only a t-shirt and jeans.

"Hey Stone, you dirty gyppo!" I called, drawing Dutch courage from his obvious problems.

"When your mum and dad see you tomorrow, lad, they won't know you!"

"You never knew your dad anyway," I shouted back.

"Little bastard!"

I ran onto the bridge, deliberately stamping on its wooden boards so that he'd have no doubt which way I'd gone. We were now at the lowest part of the Valley, and the cold was of the Arctic variety. A couple of feet below, the river was hidden by a glinting sheet of grey-green ice. It looked strong enough to support me. Briefly I was tempted. I could climb down there and back away from the bridge, shouting more insults. Stone was so enraged that he might follow – even though the ice was unlikely to hold someone as big and heavy as him. But no; for all that he was stupid, he wasn't *that* stupid. In any case, even if he did fall for it, it wouldn't be biblical enough; there'd be no poetry in such a mundane punishment. So, I crossed to the other side of the river, and started up the track towards the railway bridge and, beyond that, the farm. I was panting hard. Fit as I was, this route was steeply uphill. Again, I felt concern that Stone might stop following me, but in my thirteen-year-old innocence I was underestimating the average adult's ability to hate.

18

"Beth thinks you're joke," I shouted over my shoulder. "I heard her telling Clark the other night. She reckons you're too thick for her, said you're thick as pig-shit!"

"You little bastard!"

"She reckons your bike's crap too!"

"I'll so have you, lad!"

"If it wasn't crap before, it is now!" And I brayed with laughter.

We were ascending towards higher ground, where the mist was thinning, though it didn't dissipate entirely. Lank fingers of it lay across the frozen fields. When I reached the farm, it was like a scene from a Christmas card: the deep snow in the yard, the deeper snow on the roof, icicles hanging over mullioned windows from which a warm, rosy light emanated. Up to this point, the track had been marked by the runnels of farm vehicle tyres, but once we got onto the higher track – the one that led past the farm to Ettinshall – the snow was unbroken. It would be easier for Stone to follow my footprints, and now, I must confess, I was feeling tired and starting to wonder if maybe this hadn't been such a good idea. I was fifty yards up from the farm when I glanced back and saw him again, a dark shape still slogging in my wake. Initially when we'd set out, I'd *hoped* that he'd have this much staying power. Now that he clearly did, I was thinking it made him a more dangerous enemy than I'd anticipated. The other question nagging at me was what was I going to do next?

Blind rage had been my initial motivation when I'd finally called Stone out, so possibly I hadn't been thinking straight. But this thing *was* pre-planned. I'd brought him to this blighted spot with a strange and illogical confidence that Red Clogs would be waiting here for him. You see, I'd survived the demon's visitations twice, once in the fog last October and once during our first visit to the colliery brow in November, so it clearly wasn't me the thing was after. In addition, Father Carrickfergus's view – *"nothing in God's creation exists without a purpose"* – surely meant that what this was actually about was God's intent to smite my enemy. Again, as an adult living in a world where injustice is rampant, it's difficult to take such a notion seriously; but to a child it was real enough.

The colliery buildings loomed through the mist. They looked darker and more desolate than I'd ever imagined. A few days earlier, it would have been inconceivable that I could be up here at this time of night. For all my attempted rationalisation, it still was.

I veered away from the track leading to the main forecourt. It was wide open up there, and surely my best bet was to duck in among the ruins and try to find a hiding place. I took several passages at random, but a couple of these proved to be cluttered with rubbish, and my progress was slowed. Suppose I ran into one that proved to be a dead end? I began to panic. And then, towering above a row of buildings, I spotted the coal elevator – and I got a barmy idea. Down at the Redwater, I'd resisted the temptation to lure Stone onto the ice. How had I phrased it? – it wouldn't be "biblical enough". Well perhaps a biblical punishment was a luxury I could no longer afford. I was tiring, my second wind fading; after that long uphill trek, my legs and feet were heavy as iron, the breath wheezing in my lungs like a sawblade.

So, I stumbled around the next row of buildings onto the railway siding, and into the vaulted space beneath the elevator, where, if memory served, there was a ladder. It was black and bitterly cold under there, and I turned my ankle on the loose bricks now rendered even more treacherous by the inches of snow they were buried beneath. But yes, there *was* a ladder, just to my right-hand side. It was made from metal, but was rotted and rickety, and it swung alarmingly as I tried to climb up it. But I kept going.

Twenty feet up, I glanced back down. The gloom was nearly impenetrable, but I could just see a shape moving around. It was Stone. The moment he heard the ladder creak, he gazed up, and then he too began to climb. He was still determined to get me – that would make what I had to do easier.

I continued up, finally scrambling through a trapdoor and onto the first level. This was a rectangular platform, maybe thirty yards wide by forty. Having looked up at it several times in the past, I knew that it was incredibly dangerous; the wooden floorboards were mildewed to the point where they were ready to disintegrate, though from above, the carpet of snow would conceal that. I therefore went around its edges, only treading on the parts braced by the platform's steel frame. When I reached the far end and the next ladder, which rose up into yet more gloom, I stopped.

I didn't feel that I needed to climb any further.

Stone rose into view through the trapdoor, his breath smoking in dense clouds as though he was exhaling sulfur. He stopped at the top of the ladder and crouched to rest. His arms and face were flushed and gleaming with sweat. His muscles, pumped full of blood, looked huge. Only when he rose back to his feet did he finally speak.

"I don't know what you think you're playing at, you little runt, but you're in more trouble than you ever imagined possible."

It was unnerving that he didn't seem to be raging with anger anymore; now he was cold, matter-of-fact. He was no longer going to hammer me as a knee-jerk reaction to getting his bike trashed; now he was going to do it because he had no choice – he'd come this distance, so he had to make it worthwhile. That was my suspicion, but, either way, he was still so angry that he wasn't paying attention to his surroundings. He completely failed to spot that my footprints didn't lead across the central section of the platform, but around its outside. He plodded right into the middle of it, his hands clenching.

I remembered once saying something to Dom about how much I hated Mick Stone. At the time Dom had got defensive, clearly thinking it neat that such a menacing character was dating his sister. "Don't say anything to him, or he'll work you over," he'd advised me. "He'll batter you 'til you cry. But he won't stop then. He'll keep battering you 'til he's too tired to carry on. He'll teach you a lesson you'll never forget."

The platform collapsed.

The first we knew was a loud ripping sound – it was more like material tearing than wood splintering. And then Stone was gone; he hadn't even had time to register shock. A huge, ragged-edged hole yawned where he'd just been standing.

"And I've just taught *him* a lesson, Dom," I said, "that he won't even remember."

I edged my way back around to the ladder. When I reached it, I climbed down a few rungs until I could see his body. He was lying motionless on the snowy bricks. I waited several seconds before deciding it was safe to descend. When I got to ground level, I hesitated again. I only found the guts to approach when several clumps of snow landed on him from above and he didn't flinch. He lay half on his front, half on his side, with both arms splayed out. His face was turned towards me, so I could see that both his eyes were closed. There an immense cut across his brow, which was bleeding freely. I nudged him with my foot, but he didn't move. I nudged him even harder and still he didn't move. No surprise, I suppose – he must have fallen thirty feet.

I backed off, suddenly cold now that the sweat soaking my body was starting to chill.

Did I feel guilty?

There were so many conflicting emotions that night that it's difficult to recall exactly. Certainly, that terrible sinking sensation you used to get as a child when you knew you'd done something really bad and were certain to get caught, was absent. After all, it had been an accident. And he'd been the one chasing me; it hadn't been the other way around.

So, I set off home again, not so much pleased but quite glad that it was him on the bricks rather than me. Maybe the events of the preceding weeks had brutalised me. But we're only animals; quite often in life we're presented with a 'do it to them before they do it to you' scenario, and we usually have no problem with it. However, I clearly remember the next emotion I felt.

It was fear.

I was walking back towards the colliery forecourt through the screens when I suddenly sensed what I thought might be another presence.

I guess what really happened is that, with the threat of Mick Stone removed, all my fears and suspicions about this place came back to the fore, and it struck me hard that I was up here alone late at night. Not glancing left or right, I hurried across the hangar-like space, focusing on the dim rectangle of light that was the double doors at its far end. The mere thought of that terrible voice we'd heard the last time we were up here tempted me to run. At first, I resisted – when you run, it brings your enemy out into the open, and I wasn't sure I could handle another headlong chase. But the icy darkness around me was filled with menace, and what did I have to look forward to when I got outside again? That barren track winding between clutches of skeletal ruins, the opaque mist in the Valley bottom, another scramble through the tangled woods.

And of course, these weren't just *irrational* fears. Pete's eviscerated corpse was a vivid memory.

Good Lord, were those footsteps I could now hear? Was someone coming up behind me?

"I'm right behind you," came a singsong voice.

Or did it? Was it my fraught imagination?

I went fleetingly hysterical, spinning around to gaze into the frozen blackness. I saw nothing, but still turned back and ran hell-for-leather the remaining ten yards to the doorway – only for a silhouetted figure to step into it and block my path.

I screeched like a trapped animal. Trying to halt, I stumbled, fell, and slid forward on my knees. The figure stared silently down at me. It wasn't tall, but it was bulky and misshapen with an immense, dome-like head.

"He's back there," I wailed, jabbing a finger behind me. "I'm not supposed to be up here. *He's* the one you want, and he's back there!"

"Stephen?" a puzzled voice said.

At the best of times, Beth's voice was the sweetest sound I ever heard. But now I was overcome with joy. She drew back the big fox-fur hood she'd been wearing, but before she could do anything else, I'd jumped to my feet and grabbed her in a bear-hug of a cuddle.

"Good grief!" she said, disentangling herself. "What's the matter?"

"I'm … I'm *so* glad to see you," I stammered.

"What are you doing here? Where's Mick?"

"He was after me."

"Why was he after you?"

"I slipped on the drive and knocked his bike over. He said he was going to kill me."

She sighed. "Where is he now?"

"Around here somewhere." I shook my head with dumb innocence. "I don't know."

"Okay, give me your hand."

I wasn't a little kid, but I meekly accepted her maternal gesture – not because I was being pathetic, but because after the last few minutes it was a genuine relief to feel an adult's firm grip. And because any physical contact with Beth was desirable.

But when she added: "We need to find him," and made to head back through the screens, I resisted.

"I don't want to find him!"

"Don't worry. Nothing will happen to you while *I'm* here."

"I'm not going back through there, it's pitch-black!"

She assessed me for a moment, presumably seeing a tearful, shuddering, exhausted child – and relented. "Okay. Let's go home."

We walked hand-in-hand across the forecourt and down the track leading towards the Valley. Beth had snow-boots on, and ski pants. She was also wearing a massive winter coat, the outline of which had confused me in the dark.

"I'm not sure why, but I suspected you'd both come up here," she said. "Dom was watching from his window, and he saw Mick chasing you up Jubilee Crescent."

"Mick detests me."

"Why on Earth would he detest you?"

"Because of what happened between you and me."

"I wouldn't say something happened between us."

"You know what I mean."

She smiled to herself. "I imagine you think about that quite a lot, don't you?"

"What?"

"What you saw in my bedroom."

"No, I don't," I assured her. "Not at all, honest."

She continued to smile. "Just out of interest, how much did you actually see?"

"I dunno what you mean." I was slightly distracted, because we'd veered away from the track and seemed to be heading sideways through the ruins again.

"Yes, you do," she said, as though teasing. "How much of her did you see?"

163

"Her?"

"I mean how much of *me* did you see?"

With a shock, I realised that we were walking back down that alley between the two rows of maintenance sheds; the one with the iron gate at the far end.

"Everything, I'll bet." she added. "My lovely pert bottom, my big breasts, my beautiful pussy."

This shocked me even more. 'Pussy' was so rude a word that even we rarely got around to using it, but to hear Beth say it …? Her grip on my hand was suddenly very tight, and I saw that she was glancing around at me with a strange intensity.

"I bet that's the thing you think about most, isn't it?" she said in a voice that was hoarse, throaty, totally unlike her normal one. "My pussy … my quim … my cunt!"

I yanked my hand free, but now she grabbed my throat. Though she had woolly mittens on, I felt her fingernails bite into my flesh – it was like a cat's claw. My air supply was cut off.

"You only want one thing from her, don't you?" she spat. "Filthy little beasts like you! That's what they all want. Because she's so soft and sweet, and because she's got the face of a saint and the body of a succubus. You think you can sate your immature lusts on her, don't you? Think you can defile and degrade her! Isn't that right, you vile little monster?"

I couldn't reply because I was choking. I had her wrist with both hands, but suddenly there was no way I could break her grip. The look on her

164

face was ghastly, a combination of angelic beauty and soulless cruelty. If you can imagine a portrait of the Virgin Mary going demented, you'd be close to the mark. She slammed me backward against a brick wall. The wind was knocked out of me; my head rang.

"No-one's going to have her," she snapped. "Especially no immature little pup. As soon as she gets a pup and starts nursing it, who's going to nurse me, eh? I'll tell you, no-one. You little whelp. That's why I've brought you a new master – *this*."

I didn't know she had something in her other hand until cold metal was pressed against my face. It was only when she raised it to hit me and I saw its outline framed on the star-filled night, that I realised it was a claw-hammer.

I desperately tried to break loose. She had to struggle to hold me, but she managed it. She raised the hammer again, and then someone was onto her from behind. An arm hooked over her shoulder and down across her chest and lugged her backward.

"What're you doing … what the hell are you doing?" It was Mick Stone. His face was dry-streaked with blood and he was shaky on his feet, but he dragged her around to face him. "Beth, what the hell are you …?"

He didn't see the first blow until the hammer connected with his skull, and none of us actually heard it. Trust my personal experience when I tell you this – hammer-blows to a human body rarely make a sound. In the darkness and confusion, she'd struck him six times, savagely, before he even realised where the attack was coming from. By now he'd slumped to his knees. His freshly bloodied face was a grimace of pain.

"You've been asking for it too," she hissed. "You're a worse prospect than *he* is."

The next blow I *did* hear, because it smashed most of his teeth out, leaving his mouth a tattered, gory hole, and knocked him sideways to the ground. His knees were still beneath him, and he lay at a grisly right-angle. She kicked and stamped on his head a few times, before drawing another weapon from beneath her coat. It looked like a long, slim blade, but I later realised that it was a screwdriver. The first blow punctured the side of his throat and surely killed him – if he wasn't already dead – so the next twenty were added purely for good measure.

"*That's* for telling people you've bedded her!" she said in a crazed rythmic mantra. "*That's* for insulting her behind her back because she resisted you! *That's* for wearing her on your arm like a gold trinket! *That's* for offering her a future of nothing!"

The gloom concealed the close detail. But the snow around us turned black as she ripped and mutilated. So intent on this was she that she barely noticed I'd come round, or that I'd braced my back against the wall and was now sliding up to my feet. The gate at the end of the passage was still closed from the last time we'd been here, and I couldn't go the other way – because Beth was blocking it. The only option was to go through the sheds again. At that second, she seemed to remember I was there, and spun to glare at me. I twirled around and hurled myself through the shattered interior. She came after me, snarling like a feral thing, like a she-wolf – I swear it wasn't a human voice anymore. But it only added fuel to my terror and helped me clamber swiftly up through the broken roof and vault down over the rear wall.

In front of me, as before, lay the ruined shell that was the pit-baths.

The thought of going back in there was almost too horrible, though again there were few alternatives. To go either left or right might leave me open to ambush. So, I lurched forward, ducking through the arched entrance and staggering up the central passage. The truth is that I only managed to re-enter that place because I was so overwhelmed with the horror of other events. Did I still believe in Red Clogs at that moment? – if I did, it didn't stop me running right down to the far end of the passage, on into the shower corridor, and then into the bathroom, the very place where we'd first seen the spectre.

I knew there was another way out from here somewhere, though at this time of night it was black as a void. I collided at thigh-height with one of the cast-iron bathtubs and went staggering sideways. I crashed through the polythene curtain and fell into the heaps of broken masonry, where I groped blindly around, knowing I was making too much noise. And then, entirely fortuitously, my hand closed on something my fingers recognised – it was small, metallic and gun-shaped; the lighter Dom had dropped the last time we were here. I struck it, and a tiny flame sprang to life. There was so little fuel left that it revealed nothing except my immediate surroundings – yet this was sufficient to show two objects lying in front of me. They were old work-boots, very heavy and scuffed. And bright red.

My breath caught in my throat. My eyes almost popped from their sockets.

But they just lay there. This time they weren't attached to anyone or anything. And now that I was close to them, I began to wonder at their red sheen – which was almost too red, and at the way their laces were crusted together. Slowly it dawned on me that what I might be seeing here was not blood – but paint.

I rose to my feet and held the lighter aloft. Several feet above me, a steel bar crossed the ceiling. A piece of rope – more specifically, a piece of Gideon's blue nylon climbing-rope – was tied there. One end of it had been sliced through, as though something hanging had been cut down.

Call me a fool, but in the midst of these turbulent events I wasn't immediately able to figure it out. Only later did it occur to me that the hovering figure we saw that day when we went to collect the firewood might have been our very own Guy Fawkes. When you consider, it explained a lot – why Gideon and Charlie had been so flushed with running when they'd caught up with us by the river, and why, ever since, Gideon had been so adamant that we hadn't *really* seen Red Clogs. I hadn't noticed that the Guy we'd put on the bonfire a few days later had been missing his feet, but it would have been sensible for Gideon and Charlie to remove them beforehand so as not to reveal the trick they'd played.

As I say, at this moment I was too frightened to work this out. I merely backed away from the boots and searched for the exit. This was a single door standing ajar by about three inches. Before going out, I glanced back. The green-stained polythene curtain obscured much of the rest of the room. I imagined a figure just beyond it, watching me. But no shape stirred on the other side; there was no sound. Relieved, I flicked the lighter off, and, as quietly as I could, opened the door and slipped outside.

That was where she was waiting.

I was moving quickly, so the hammer only struck me a glancing blow, but it was behind my right ear and it stunned me. I tottered forward and fell. My face hit virgin snow, and this revived me a little. But I was only able to roll over onto my back before she came and stood over me. As well as the hammer, she also held the screwdriver. Her face was hidden beneath her darkened hood, but dragon-breath steamed out of her. She raised both weapons, as if planning to attack me with them simultaneously. It might seem ridiculous, but in what looked like the last moment of my life, I remembered those other words of Father Carrickfergus: *"Jesus is always there, walking alongside us."*

I almost laughed. If Jesus *was* walking alongside me, now would be the time for him to show his hand. At which point I heard a low, fluting whistle, followed by a dull *thud*.

Beth jerked forward slightly.

All she said was: "Oh."

When she turned to look behind her, I saw a long, slender shaft protruding from the middle of her back. I didn't at first realise what it was, but then I heard a second whistle and a second *thud*, and I realised that another shaft had struck her. I was lying at such an angle that I saw it slam into her lower ribs, perhaps sinking in a couple of inches.

"Oh," she said again. "Oh … oh, my goodness." And this time it was Beth speaking – in that unmistakably gentle voice. "Oh … Dominic, what have you done?"

Dom came into view, wearing his Parka and bob-cap, a third arrow already knocked to his bowstring. Even from this distance, I could see that his eyes were glistening with tears. He said something to her, but I couldn't quite tell what it was because it came out blubbered; it was something like: "Mum's been reading the papers, she knows – she said I had to watch you."

"Dominic," Beth said again, sounding disappointed "What … what've you done?"

"It's what you've done!" he cried – and it was a shrill, childish cry, almost a squawk.

He didn't fire his third arrow, possibly because he'd only brought three, but it was drawn at full string, and he pointed it towards her as he advanced. Beth was already badly hurt. She took an unsteady step backward, and then another. I tried to get out of the way, but it was too late: she tripped over me and fell full length, and, with a sickening *crack*, the first arrow was driven clean through her torso.

She made no sound but arched and twisted in torturous pain. I took the opportunity to crawl away, but she clawed out at me and grabbed my jacket. I tried futilely to pry myself free; she used me to drag herself back up into a sitting position and came face-to-face with me. Her hood had fallen back and briefly she was something from a Hammer vampire movie: the long dark hair, the feline beauty, the little-girl-lost expression daubed with fresh blood, and the tip of the cruel barb that had pierced her heart jutting out between fulsome breasts.

"St … Stephen," she whispered, more blood frothing from her lips, "… look after him, yes? Please … look after him …"

Her mouth twisted into a smile, and again with cat-like speed, her hand moved to my throat, clamping it hard. I gargled and struggled, and there was a *twang* of wire and something flashed past my ear, piercing her again, this time through the throat. Her grip was broken, and I rolled away as she dropped backward into the snow, twitching convulsively.

When I jumped to my feet, Dom had already thrown the bow down. Both his hands were balled into fists as he banged them against his eyes. His teeth were clenched so tightly on his bottom lip that blood dribbled down his chin. He keened like a wounded animal as I hared past him, taking the path downhill towards the farmhouse.

I'd almost made it to the farm front door, when I heard him start to howl.

19

It was a complete revelation to me, and to everyone else in Ashburn, that Mrs. Blyford was still alive and dwelling in an institute for the criminally insane.

Apparently, she'd been held there for the last ten years, having voluntarily taken the blame for the murder of a neighbouring two-year-old. Her husband was the one who'd certified her insanity. In fact, he'd connived with her all the way down the line, diagnosing a kind of extreme and completely bogus post-natal depression. Rather than see their nine-year-old daughter incarcerated, he and his wife had opted for what they'd considered the lesser of two evils. After that, they'd hushed the whole thing up. Doctor Blyford had brought his family seventy miles south to Lancashire, where the three boys had been raised under strict orders never to mention that their mother was still alive because of the disgrace it would bring, though they would sometimes go to visit her, hence Dom's occasional day-long absences.

As for Beth, again at Doctor Blyford's contrivance, she'd been sent to a succession of special schools for disturbed children, ostensibly because she was damaged by the experience of seeing her mother murder the little boy from next door, but in reality, because he'd detected that she suffered from a split-personality disorder.

She'd returned home in 1974 not because she'd been cured, but because Doctor Blyford had aged prematurely over the previous decade – for long, long years he'd been tormented by the knowledge of his terrible deception and his wife's voluntary suffering – and as such his work had declined, his private practise had diminished, and soon he could no longer afford luxuries. The upkeep of his house had thus deteriorated, Dom had had to leave public school, and Beth was sent home. She'd never been sectioned – it was only Doctor Blyford's regular cheques that had kept her under constant observation, so when the fees ran out there was no reason why she shouldn't be released to the custody of her family.

Needless to say, it was a sensational case. It made all the papers for two weeks. I became a minor celebrity in the town, especially at school, where, after coming out of hospital, I returned to a hero's welcome. But when I look back on it, there were clues that even a youngster like me should have picked up on: the ease with which robust, red-blooded lads had been lured out of sight; the *clinking* footsteps that followed me through the fog – almost exactly the same sound that Beth's high heels made when she walked on paving stones; the fact that she'd bought herself a new pair of plimsoles only a few days after Pete had been kicked to death; the fact that Dom, after his mother had warned him during his latest visit, had repeatedly attempted to ingratiate himself with Beth – possibly because he didn't want to believe what he'd been told about her, though, looking back on it, he was actually behaving like a brutalised wife who fawns and fusses over her abusive husband in the hope it will avert another attack.

I never saw Dom again.

He wouldn't speak to me before his father's trial, and afterwards he and his family left the area. Ultimately, Doctor Blyford was sent to prison and his wife was released. She sold the house and moved with her children to some other part of the country (Colin Lapwing thought it was Devon, though God knows how he was supposed to know). Beth was cremated during a private ceremony, and her ashes interred in the municipal cemetery in the centre of town. On the paving stone beneath which she lies there is a simple brass plate. It reads:

A loving daughter, long lost

Strange to say, but for me life was more or less back to normal by Christmas. Other things were soon in the news. Seventeen people had been massacred in an IRA bomb outrage in Birmingham; Lord Lucan, who was on the run for murdering his child's nanny, was being spotted everywhere; and runaway inflation was about to knock Britain's economy for six. Of course, as a child, things like that pass over you. It astonishes me now, but I look back on the Christmas of 1974 and remember enjoying it as much as any other. Snow fell on and off all through the holiday period, which enhanced the atmosphere. Possibly because of my experiences, I received oodles more presents that year, as did my sister, Sarah. On Christmas Day morning, I knelt waist-deep in festive wrappers, my attention torn between my new Chopper bike, my new record player complete with albums by *Slade*, *The Sweet* and *Gary Glitter*, and my new collection of box games: *Haunted House*, *Movie Maker*, *Mousetrap*.

It probably helped block out the reality of what had happened. But one question remained unanswered, and even now – in my late forties – I ponder it and feel confused. It concerns those red boots in the pit-baths, the ones I glimpsed on the night Beth chased me, the ones just lying there. It seems obvious now that they'd belonged to the Guy Fawkes (Gideon and his mischievous mate having painted them red to scare us). But after Colin Lapwing's school outburst, the police had searched the pithead area with dogs, including the baths, and had found no such objects. Likewise, after Beth died, and the entire colliery brow became a crime scene, they searched again – and still didn't find them.

I never spoke to Gideon or Charlie again, so I didn't get a chance to ask them what the truth was. But to my knowledge, no-one has ever found those red boots.

Was it paint that covered them? It looked like it, but I was only thirteen – would I know?

These days, Ettinshall Colliery has gone, and new housing estates cover that once blighted hillside. At night, you can see lots of lights up there – streetlights, house lights, the headlights of cars. But there are dark patches as well; places you can't see into no matter how hard you try, especially at night: behind garages, beside sheds, beneath hedges. I wouldn't drive up there alone, never mind walk. But wherever I am now, I'm always careful while walking alone – especially when the leaves are falling, and the days are short, and the season of mist is upon us.